MW00584560

Also by Laura van den Berg

STATE
OF
PARADISE

STATE
OF
PARADISE

A NOVEL

Laura van den Berg

Farrar, Straus and Giroux
New York

Farrar, Straus and Giroux
120 Broadway, New York 10271

Printed in the United States of America
First edition, 2024

Library of Congress Cataloging-in-Publication Data
Names: Van den Berg, Laura, author.
Title: State of paradise: a novel / Laura van den Berg.
Description: First edition. | New York: Farrar, Straus and
    Giroux, 2024.
Identifiers: LCCN 2023057436 | ISBN 9780374612207
    (hardcover)
Subjects: LCGFT: Novels.
Classification: LCC PS3622.A58537 S73 2024 |
    DDC 813/.6—dc23/eng/20231218
LC record available at https://lccn.loc.gov/2023057436

Designed by Gretchen Achilles

Our books may be purchased in bulk for promotional,
educational, or business use. Please contact your local bookseller
or the Macmillan Corporate and Premium Sales Department at
1-800-221-7945, extension 5442, or by email at
MacmillanSpecialMarkets@macmillan.com.

www.fsgbooks.com
Follow us on social media at @fsgbooks

1   3   5   7   9   10   8   6   4   2

For Caroline & CJ

Art is where what we survive survives.

—KAVEH AKBAR, "THE PALACE"

THE WILDERNESS

MAY 15–JULY 1

Knives

In Florida, my husband runs. Ten miles a day, seventy miles a week, a physical feat that is astonishing to me. He started running after he got stuck on a book he is trying to write, a historical account of pilgrimages in medieval Europe. Back then it was not unusual for pilgrims to traverse hundreds of miles on foot: 248 miles from Bologna to the catacombs in Rome; 500 from Mannheim to Our Lady of Walsingham. My husband is a trained historian and fascinated by journeys. He wants to understand what has become of the pilgrimage in our broken modern world. In the meantime, he observes a lot on his daily voyages. For example, there has been an increase in carrion birds down by the lake. Cobalt crows circling overhead, bloodstains on the sidewalk, awaiting the erasure of afternoon rain. He returns so sweat-wet it looks like he's been swimming. He returns overflowing with story. When a story is told to another person it takes on a life of its own; it spreads, contagion-like. The more times a story is shared the more powerful it becomes. This morning my husband witnessed a man—a neighborhood regular who gets around on a bike, a white dog with caramel ears trotting along beside him—ride up to a truck parked by the lake. An unsheltered community sleeps in cars and campers in this area; in the aftermath of the pandemic, the population tripled, with blue tents pitched in the park. My

husband has seen the owner of this particular truck, a man
with a white beard, drinking morning beers on his tailgate
and looking askance at the world. Today the bike man rested
one foot on the ground, looked left and then right. He pulled
a knife from his pants pocket and jammed the blade into the
truck's back tire. The truck man was asleep inside (my husband could see him slumped against the window, the swirl
of white hair, the bleached denim jacket sleeve) and did not
stir. The dog sat perfectly still as the tire hissed and withered.
As the bike man withdrew the blade, he looked up at my
husband jogging in place. He tipped the blade, like a cowboy
in an old western, and then he tucked the knife back into his
pants pocket and rode on. Now my husband thinks he and
the bike man have entered into some kind of pact—a vow
of silence. That evening, we take our dog for a walk and pass
the bike man and his white dog resting on the shaded steps
of a blue brick church. I think about the knife hidden somewhere on the bike man's body, sharp enough to tear through
a tire. I wonder what the truck man did to deserve the knif-
ing. Maybe nothing. Everyone, it seems, is more desperate
than they were before. I wonder where the bike man and his
dog sleep at night. On the church steps? In the park? We
have been in Florida, land of my childhood, since the start
of the year, living in my mother's house. Now we stand on
the threshold of summer's sweltering cave. During the pandemic I got sick but recovered after a week of rolling around
in a wet fever. Ever since, I've had the strangest dreams. Is
it possible for a fever to turn a body so hot that molecules

are rearranged? Is our life just on pause or is this pause now our life? The white dog barks. Our dog barks back. Twice for good measure. I wonder what they are saying to each other, in their animal language. All the people wave.

In Florida, I am a writer, though not a real one. I ghost for a very famous thriller author. When I first got the job, I spent a month reading books by the famous author, to better understand the task that lay before me. The chapters were always short; the sentences never had too many words. The phrase *everything is not as it seems* appeared in nearly all the book descriptions. Whenever I'm stuck on a chapter, I just write *everything is not as it seems* and press on. In my line of work, this phrase is like hot sauce or ranch dressing—you can put it on nearly everything. Ghostwriting is a largely unregulated industry. We are the animating force behind many a celebrity memoir and blockbuster detective series. Some ghosts regard themselves as "collaborators." They lobby for cover credit. Interviews, press. Others like the idea of being invisible. It is the act of vanishing that attracts them to the work in the first place. Other ghosts—such as myself—are paid just well enough to write our chapters and keep our mouths shut. We are like the staff of a country estate: we keep the place running and we are meant to blend into the background. Ghosting is not how I intended to spend my days on this earth, but the world feels precarious and so I struggle to break free from the job. I belong to a fleet of ghosts and have never actually corresponded with the famous author himself. I often imagine him wandering a castle in a silk bathrobe in some small cold country—Switzerland, Austria—and slicing the air with a silver letter opener as he concocts his plots, even though I know the author lives in a mansion down in Palm Beach. From the famous author's team of assistants, I get templates of scenes, and then it's up to me to fill in the details. Paint-by-numbers writing. My current project is about a retired cop—bereaved and semi-alcoholic, traits that are supposed to make him "complicated" yet "sympathetic"—who gets sucked back into the Miami underworld after he finds millions of dollars' worth of cocaine washed up on a beach. When I finish a chapter, I send it on to the assistants, who weed out anything of myself that I might have tried to smuggle in. If I submit chapters that are too well written—too descriptive, too vulnerable, too precise—the assistants become upset, tell me to cut the flourishes. They want the language to do the opposite of what language should do, which is leave a mark. They want the language to be forgettable, familiar, digestible. To enter into the reader and disappear without a trace.

My mother lives in a small town northeast of Orlando, surrounded by a lush network of rivers and lakes. My sister lives next door, even though the two of them have never gotten along. They accuse each other of being moody, self-absorbed, generally unreasonable. Now, if they want to argue, all they have to do is shout at each other through an open window or over the backyard fence. They don't even have to leave their property or pick up the phone. Because my husband and I currently live with my mother, my sister often assumes we've taken her side. "I feel like I'm in an asylum," my husband said when we first arrived—and then caught himself because there is only one of us who knows for real what it's like to live in an asylum and that person would be me. In this town, the street numbers rise when you travel south, fall when you go north. We are smack between Orlando and Daytona Beach, encircled by hardwood hammocks and cypress swamps, wetlands and salt marshes. A wilderness. The Tarzan movies of the 1930s were filmed around here. A rummage shop in town sells replicas of the vintage film posters. In one Tarzan grips a bowie knife. The rummage shop is next door to the offices for the local newspaper. During the pandemic, a couple in a white RV moved into the parking lot. Back then we only left the house to buy food, and through the car window I would see them sitting around oil stains in pink plastic beach chairs, smoking or taking a nap with magazines covering their faces. Casual as can be, even though all around them tens of thousands of people were getting sick and dying. Eventually the quarantine ended and our governor, who bears a striking resemblance to a Cro-Magnon in a suit, told us that the emergency was over and everything would return to how it was before. Shortly after the governor's announcement the RV vanished. Every time I pass the parking lot for the local newspaper I wonder where those people have gone.

. . .

The newspaper has an advice column, Ask Ava. In ancient times, pilgrims journeyed to the Temple of Apollo, to consult the Oracle of Delphi on vital matters, even though the Oracle was known for inscrutable replies. I wonder if Ava regards herself as a modern-day Oracle. Today's letter writer is seeking counsel about a friend, a woman she's known for years. During the quarantine, the friend started texting her photos late at night. In each one, she looked more and more like the letter writer. She cropped her hair and dyed it black. She ordered new clothes and makeup. She tweezed her eyebrows into skinny arches. After the governor announced that the pandemic had been defeated, the two women went out to lunch and the letter writer said it was like sitting across from a slightly different version of herself. The friend even wore the exact same T-shirt, mint green with a pink pineapple on the front. *Like she's been in my head.* The letter writer is worried that her description of this situation makes her sound unhinged. Perhaps she is the one who has suffered a psychological collapse. All those hours spent alone during the quarantine, watching the news and doomscrolling and getting lost in MIND'S EYE, a virtual reality meditation device made by ELECTRA, a Miami-based tech company. Nevertheless, she has her friend's transformation saved, photo by photo, on her phone. One night she was watching TV and glimpsed a face—more specifically the face of her friend, which now looked a lot like her own self—filling her living room window like a small, round moon. After that, she started carrying a pocketknife. I am frankly surprised Ava has taken this one on. It seems like a lot for an advice columnist to handle. Ava says that some people are like cosmic vacuums, always searching for other selves to consume. She advises the letter writer to sever the friendship and believes the friend will simply move on to another host. I want to ask Ava if she's ever seen *Single White Female* or *Fatal Attraction*. What if the breakup doesn't take? *Good luck with this one!* Ava says.

Once, I took a self-defense class for women. The class was held in a one-room studio in a strip mall. Dingy white walls. A toilet that wouldn't stop running. Our main task was to fend off a man with a rubber knife. The man would rush up behind us and press the blade to our throats and say something menacing like *bitch, you're coming with me*. Next the instructor would walk us through how to escape. First, shrug your shoulders to your ears. Second, grab the attacker's wrists. Third, yank the attacker's arms down while also hurling your own weight toward the floor. But don't sit! You want to stay standing so you can run away. In the event of an actual attack, the odds of us remembering this sequence seemed very low. Still, we all gamely struggled from one step to the next until the fake attacker—who, in my judgment, seemed to take a little too much pleasure in saying *bitch, you're coming with me*—gave in and released us. The last woman to attempt escape did not follow these instructions. Instead she made fists and bent her arms like she was sitting down in a chair. Next she rammed the points of her elbows into the fake attacker's ribs. He dropped the knife and staggered backward, as if he were the one who'd been stabbed. When it was time for her to run, she didn't just do a sad lap around the classroom, like the rest of us. She bolted out the door and into the parking lot and she did not come back. We gathered around the windows and watched her figure grow smaller and smaller, her long brown ponytail trailing behind her like the tail of a kite. *That woman had freakishly pointy elbows*, the instructor told us. *Like knives, those elbows. That move would not work for a regular person, with nonlethal elbows, just so you know.* I learned a lot from the class, though none of it came from the instructor. For example, I learned that once you start running it can be hard to stop.

In Florida, a summer storm can feel like the end of the world is being summoned. These storms roll in most afternoons, which is to say there is a regular feeling of apocalypse. The clouds turn a dense ash black, as though nightfall has arrived hours ahead of schedule. Lightning that looks like it means to split the sky. Thunder that will make a glass tremble on a table. Blue blasts of rain. The windows leak rainwater; dirt levitates in the backyard. Hail sails down through the green boughs of trees, leaves spiderwebs on car windshields, smashes roof shingles. We watch our reflections melt and twist in the rain-soaked windows. This weather passes so quickly I'll look outside and can't be sure if I dreamed the ferocious storm or its flat blue aftermath, which is exactly how I felt during the pandemic, after I emerged from that fevered week, unsure if the flat blue aftermath was *real life* or if *real life* was lost forever and the world I was stepping into now was nothing more than a long, strange dream.

During one of these afternoon storms our phones hum with tornado warnings. "Where do we go?" my husband asks my mother, who is reading Francis Bacon's incomplete utopian novel, *New Atlantis*, in the living room. "Anywhere but out-side," she replies. My mother has taken an interest in utopian texts, now that Florida seems to be heading in the opposite direction, though every time she describes one of these alleged paradises they sound a little terrifying. Too much manual labor and religious fervor. In the end, my mother often seems disappointed by these utopias too; she is still searching for her true north. My husband, meanwhile, is disturbed that my mother's house does not have a single windowless room. Unlike my childhood home, which had a basement. The concrete bottom shimmered with water and rats scratched out nests in the stucco walls. My father was always scattering green pellets of rat poison on the wood staircase. The house was very old and I had to venture down there periodically to flip the circuit breakers. I never used a flashlight, because I was too scared to see what was writhing around in the water below. I took one step at a time with my arms extended, fingers curling around the shadows, the poison pellets crunching under my shoes. I can remember feeling as though all the volatility in our house was alive in the water and the walls, luring me closer. So basements in Florida are a frightful thing even if they do give you a place to shelter during a tornado. I text my sister, to ask what she thinks we should do, but she doesn't reply until the storm is at full blast. *Sorry*, she says. *I was meditating.* During the pandemic, my sister became addicted to MIND'S EYE, to putting on her white headset and sliding down into other worlds. During the quarantine, ELECTRA representatives got special permission to drive all over the state and leave free headsets on doorsteps. An alleged act of public service, to help people cope with the isolation, but still there was something strange about a black van parking in the middle of the street and unleashing a small flood of masked ELECTRA employees, each holding a white pyramid of shrink-wrapped headsets. *Don't take a shower*, my sister advises. *Or wash any dishes.* This particular storm is a tropical system and has some staying power. My mother continues to read Francis Bacon undisturbed as the lights flicker and paintings shudder on the walls. All night my husband and I listen to the lashing rain, to the lightning that summons a cracking brightness. Our dog stands on the foot of the bed and growls. Like there are forces he wants to keep out. In the morning, I walk the dog on wet sidewalks papered with green leaves. Together we leap over fallen branches that look like the severed arms of giants. At an intersection, a white car blows through a stop sign. The windows are fogged; I hear screaming inside. The passenger door swings open and a woman in a denim skirt and a black tank top hurls herself—or is hurled—onto the street. I start in her direction, pulling the panting dog along behind me. "Hey," I call out to her. "Are you okay?" The woman turns from the car and races down an alley, a skinny dirt path that cuts between the rows of houses. I don't get a look at the driver before they flee, the open passenger door swinging wildly. By the time we reach the alley the woman is gone. "Be careful going out after storms," my mother advises when we get home. "People get electrocuted by downed wires all the time." The news is reporting that the tornado inhaled roofs and flattened fences in neighboring towns. I watch shaky camera footage of a man surveying his vanquished lawn. All the windows have been blown out; the roof is gone. In what used to be a living room the furniture is now a smashed heap of debris. I seek out what is still recognizable: a lampshade, a cracked TV screen. The man's father in a wheelchair, shaking his fist at the heavens above. The soaking red of police lights, which make me think only of the visitation of terror, as opposed to the promise of relief, despite what the books I ghostwrite would have you believe. The absence of panes and shingles, that armor against the elements, reveals the house for what it really is—a frame, an outline, a tender suggestion of shape. I get a garbage bag and a rake and collect the branches from my mother's yard. Strange things surface in the dirt after a big storm. A green plastic kazoo. A blue lighter. A metal dog tag, faded and bone-shaped, the lettering inscrutable. A pearl button. Where have these objects been hiding? I imagine a cave system underneath my mother's yard, kidney-shaped caverns filled with colorful plastic toys. Today with the rake I uncover a white porcelain knob, cut clean in half, as though severed by a very sharp knife.

A place outside time. This is the phrase I overhear my husband using as he tries to describe Florida to his father over the phone. His father lives in a high-rise condo in New Jersey, and he is concerned that we are still down here. On the news, there is constant talk about Florida's post-pandemic spiral. Speculation about whether the state is experiencing an ecological and spiritual succession. There is talk about militias creeping out of the swamp. There is talk of vandals. There is talk of literal highway robbery. (Our Cro-Magnon governor denies any of this is happening, even though there are reports that some of these forces are amassing in his name.) For the time being, I can ghostwrite my books and shop specials at the grocery and take my niece to the water park, but no one knows how much longer this version of our world will last. "Sometimes I can't believe a place like this exists," my husband says as we speed down a gleaming white limestone road that cuts through a palm forest, or ride an airboat around a swollen lake. Florida has a past, as all places do, but these days everyone is uncertain about its future.

Here are some facts, from when I lived here last.

• • •

Days that felt like they'd been drenched in tar. Two attempts, one experimental and one sincere. One hospitalization, in Fort Lauderdale. During my time at the Institute, I saw and experienced things I have never discussed with another human soul. A pact of silence I have made with myself. This all happened nearly two decades ago and I have lived many other lives since then, and yet the feeling of being lost in a vast wilderness—wandering and wandering until you get so tired all you want is to lie down and sleep—is never far.

In the year before I moved away from Florida, I spent hours in the all-night Denny's with my best friend at the time, a girl I'd met in an outpatient therapy group, eating pancakes and discussing our plans for self-annihilation like two criminals plotting the heist of a lifetime. Secretly I had decided that I wanted to live, and somehow talking about death with another person made the prospect of it feel further away. Turned it into a story we could not stop telling. Then I was, to my great surprise, admitted to a doctoral program in literature, all the way up in Boston. I was twenty-two and I had only ever lived in Florida. I had not told this girl, or anyone else, that I'd even applied. Stealing away like a thief in the night seemed like the only way to go, although now, all these years later, Florida has figured out a way to call me back. My best friend felt betrayed by my sudden departure and so we stopped speaking. Because I had resolved to leave the wilderness I'd assumed that she would find her way out too. Desperation can make people mercenary like that—you spot an exit and you start running toward it and you don't look back. You just do your best to convince yourself that the other person is right behind you. Several years ago, I learned, from a mutual friend, that this other girl did not make it out. Only by the time the wilderness took her she was not a girl but a woman, married with children. I did not ask how she did it. If she used a weapon. A knife. Which used to be integral to her master plan back when we were still young. It was around this time that I started to wonder if the wilderness is not something a person can choose to leave. Rather it is a place that lives inside us. A landscape with its own intelligence and design.

I left Florida to become a student of literature, which I did not enjoy as much as I had anticipated. For one thing, I struggled to understand my classmates, who all knew how to style winter scarves. Each time I tried to wear a winter scarf I felt like I was being strangled. I met my husband in a university lecture hall. At the time, he was on his way to becoming a doctor of history, and by chance we both attended a talk on Yevgeny Zamyatin's *We*, a novel about a mathematician living in a futuristic city made entirely of glass apartment buildings. The character's best friend is a state-sponsored poet who recites his work at public executions, and his lover is a spy for the

Bureau of Guardians. The mathematician is the chief engineer for a spaceship, built for the purpose of colonizing other planets. He starts a journal with the hope it can be smuggled onto the completed spaceship. That some small part of him can escape. *We* was written in the early 1920s, and yet as I listened to the lecturer discuss the themes I did not feel like I was in the presence of something very old or something that existed in an inconceivable future, but rather a reality that I might meet in my lifetime. It was snowing outside; the lecture hall windows looked like they were covered by white curtains. The man I would end up marrying was sitting next to me and he was not wearing a scarf. His copy of *We* was open and I noticed one passage had been heavily underlined, with little stars drawn in the margins. "What's that?" I whispered, poking him in the arm, and he slid the book over in my direction. *The knife is the most durable, immortal, the most genius thing that man created. The knife was the guillotine; the knife is the universal means of solving all knots; and along the blade of a knife lies the path of paradox—the single most worthy path of the fearless mind.* I had forgotten to bring my copy of *We* to the lecture, so the book stayed between us. Afterward, we walked to a coffee shop, sliding around in the snowy streets. Before long, we had merged our paltry furniture into a rented apartment and undertaken a life of domestic contentment that I had not ever imagined would be available to me. In the end, I never finished my dissertation, despite spending years slogging through coursework. I arrived at the realization that I did not want to spend my life writing about books that had already been written; rather, I wanted to write stories that did not yet exist. My adviser thought this was a mistake. "Writers would be nothing without us," he sniffed. My husband did succeed in becoming a doctor of history, and after he finished his degree we moved from one city to another for his teaching jobs. I liked this itinerant life; so long as I stayed in motion I thought the wilderness would never catch me. When I landed the ghostwriting job, I told myself that becoming a ghost at least got me closer to my goal than a dissertation on Chaucer. Technically speaking I was participating in the creation of books that did not yet exist, even if they were not stories that I myself had imagined or would ever have chosen to tell.

Wildlife

In Florida, I count cats. I first started counting the cats—a mix of strays and outdoor pets with collars and bells—while walking the dog and soon realized that we are hopelessly surrounded. Cats lounge on driveways and front lawns, crouch like gargoyles on porch railings and fence posts, lurk in the bushes and under cars and behind trees, peer out from underneath crawl spaces. The derelict houses in the neighborhood appear to have been overtaken by cats—they crowd the decaying front porches, use the walls as scratching posts—and nearly all the non-derelict houses have what my husband and I refer to as a "stoop cat." My husband is interested in acquiring a stoop cat of our own and I keep trying to explain to him that if we want a stoop cat we'll have to leave food out, that there is no such thing as a free stoop cat, but he is nervous that such an offering will attract rats (he is sure he's seen rodents rustling around in the tawny heads of palm trees). My husband is nervous about a lot of things down here, like the monstrous size of the fire ants and the quality of the gasoline, because half the time the gas stations are out, the nozzles bundled up in black garbage bags, or the credit card readers don't work or the attendant is a shirtless man with a hip flask tucked into the waistband of his shorts. I keep trying to explain that this is a place with its own laws. Meanwhile, my old rhythms are flooding back: how to trap lizards with mason jars; walking the dog in a sports bra and cutoffs; dropping letters from my sentences when I greet people on the street. I feel like I am meeting a version of myself that I had nearly forgotten. The version that I tried to ditch on my way out of the wilderness. The version that emerged when the pandemic fever passed and I realized I wasn't dead. She feels a bit dangerous, this version. I suspect she's been waiting on me all these years, like a scorpion curled up inside the heel of a boot. One morning, I'm walking the dog and I hear a hissing sound right above my head. A black cat perched in a neighbor's arbor, flashing its teeth from behind white sprigs of star jasmine. I have no superstitions about black cats. I've started taking photos of the cats with my phone, which they do not appreciate. When the camera appears they look away, flick their tails, spring up and shoot underneath a house, dive into some brush. Save for this one cat that stared right into the camera, orange and royal as a lion. A few nights later, on an evening walk with my dog, we pass ten cats, all stretched out in the scorched crabgrass behind a neighbor's back door. They watch us as we pass, their furred heads turning slowly at the same time. They look like they are casually dreaming of murder. Like they are guarding a portal to the underworld. Like they have been alive since the dawn of earth.

On Nextdoor, cats never seem to meet a good end. A woman writes a post about how she believes a man in a truck is abducting loose cats and relocating them to remote areas.

A different woman writes about finding the front half of a black cat in her yard, perfectly intact. She does not think this is the work of an animal, wild or domestic. She thinks someone is trying to threaten her, or is practicing witchcraft.

Sometimes I dream that all these cats live in the castle with the famous thriller author who employs me. The cats like the weather in the small, cold country, just as they like the chilly stone and the velvet chaise longues inside. In my dreams, the cats are the ones who come up with all the book ideas. They stand on their hind legs and dictate the plots to the author—*how about an FBI agent who is forced into early retirement by a medical allergy to sunlight but must return to the field when her past threatens to catch up with her as it ALWAYS DOES. Humans never learn, which is what makes these books so amusing to us. All the scenes would have to take place at night, of course . . . we'll call this one THE MIDNIGHT CURE.* In my dreams, the famous author is less king of the castle than a prisoner in a garret, barricaded in a room with all these cats purring nonstop with ideas. He types like a man rowing a boat in the shadow of a tidal wave.

The number of cats is rivaled only by the number of lizards. Summer is the season of the lizard. In the winter, they will go dormant, but for now we are overrun. Common garden lizards, brown and green anoles about the length of a human finger, toothless and harmless, and yet I'm on constant alert, steeling myself for the jump scare of yanking back the shower curtain and finding a lizard clinging to the white tile or waking to a lizard perched atop the stack of books on my nightstand, fanning its crimson dewlap. Today I'm drinking coffee and writing a chapter at the kitchen table when a lizard leaps right out of my hair. My husband says he feels like he's an extra in *Jurassic Park* except someone has turned all the dinosaurs miniature. In Florida, nature is seductive and full of vengeance. To live here is to engage in a ceaseless battle to keep the outdoors from coming in, but in this instance there is absolutely nothing to do but admit defeat: there are hundreds of thousands of lizards out there, with bodies malleable enough to slip through the smallest crack. This is why it's important to know how to catch lizards in mason jars, so we can help them rejoin the countless hordes outside. My mother's backyard is so full of lizards that the grass undulates of its own accord. Once, when I was talking to my sister through the backyard fence, I witnessed a lizard drop from a tree branch and onto the blond back of my dog, who was galloping across the yard in hot pursuit of a tennis ball. My sister was telling me about an article she'd just read on the founder of ELECTRA. Little is known, because the founder does not appear in public, but they are rumored to be a man, a college dropout, an orphan, a libertarian, a mad genius with possibly malevolent intentions. In the MIND'S EYE device, there are no hand controls. The device scans the user's iris, opens a line of communication between consciousness and machine. After that process is complete, the movements through the virtual world are guided by the user's thoughts. Or: *the thoughts under your thoughts.* That was the language the founder used, in a press release. The founder says that MIND'S EYE is not in the business of augmenting reality; it exists to transport, transform. *Go where you need to be*: that is their slogan. There are, of course, parameters—you cannot think *let a million dollars rain down from the sky* and just expect it to happen—but no one knows what the parameters are or what is meant by *the thoughts under your thoughts* or what will happen if *going where you need to be* leads you to a place you don't like at all. These open questions lend the device a certain allure. I never tried MIND'S EYE, because the last thing I want is a mad genius with questionable intentions poking around in my head. *You spend too much time in that thing*, I told my sister through the fence. *I wish you would try it so you could understand*, my sister replied. *I wish you weren't so fearful of technology.* In the backyard, the lizard held fast to my dog's coat, rode him like a horse.

When my classmates at the doctoral program asked about my Florida wildlife stories I knew they were expecting reptile yarns, and while I certainly have those stories to tell (the racer snake coiled like a massive shit in the toilet, the alligator sunbathing in the backyard), I always preferred to take them by surprise. When I was a little girl, my father brought a wolf home. This is not a metaphor. He took my half brother, who is older than me, on a road trip through the American West. For a month, they traveled around in a camper van. In Colorado, my father discovered an ad for wolf cubs in a local newspaper. They drove out to see the litter, at a rural address outside Grand Junction. They found a stark lot with a double-wide on a hill and a cedar tree with a heavy chain looped around the trunk. From the grooves in the copper dirt it was clear a large animal had been tethered there, clawing at the soil. A woman in work coveralls and a baseball cap stood tall by the tree, as imposing as the landscape. She had one cub she hadn't yet sold, a silver female; she said that if the cub didn't find a buyer soon she'd have to drown her. During the drive back to Florida, my half brother carried the silver female in the pouch of his sweatshirt. They bought cartons of milk at gas stations. They fed the cub with a turkey baster. My half brother can remember drifting off in the passenger seat and waking to the sensation of the wolf cub sucking on his finger—the wet mouth, the pricking teeth. In the story my father would later tell, he knew they were being hustled by the woman in the coveralls, but my half brother had begged and begged. In my half brother's version, it was my father who went misty-eyed at the mention of drowning. No one expressed any concern that I might be eaten when they returned.

In Florida, the wolf grew and grew. She was rangy and silver, with a black dot at the base of her tail and long canines. Paws the size of salad plates. She bayed at the moon, which caused problems with the neighbors, as did the disappearance of several area cats. If Nextdoor had existed in the eighties, I can only imagine the posts that would have been written about us. She spent most of her time pacing in the backyard, like if she just kept walking eventually she could get back to where she belonged. She made trenches so deep she was only half-visible when inside them; it looked like she was slowly disappearing into the earth. I have yet to dream about my father, now that he's dead, but I've had many dreams about the wolf, about a creature so deep in her trench that her silver head appears to be floating.

On occasion, the wolf would pause, raise her big silver head, and stare through the window—or at least that's what she appeared to be doing. I would wonder if she was seeing her own reflection, warped by the afternoon sunlight, or if she was able to make out my face through the illuminated glass. If she wondered what kind of creature I was.

Everyone who's heard the wolf story has fallen into two categories: those who ask what happened to the wolf, in the end, and those who do not.

After a year, my parents gave her to some friends, a couple who lived on a farm near Lake City. Green fields, rolling hills—as much as hills can roll in Florida. Apparently these friends had visited us one weekend and taken a shine to the wolf. They offered to adopt her, and my parents reasoned the wolf would be more at peace in the countryside. This sounds like a happy ending except for one thing: whenever I pressed my parents, in later years, about how the wolf fared in Lake City, they would claim to not know. "So you give these friends a wolf and you never hear from them again?" I would ask. "Maybe we did get updates and we just don't remember," they would say. "After all, this happened a long time ago." Which is true enough: this *did* happen a long time ago. My parents were still married. My half brother was in high school. I was a little girl. My younger sister was not yet born. Still, the lack of information has always left me feeling unsettled, suspicious. The wolf lived happily ever after in the countryside! The end! Such a clean, closed door. Later I would wonder if something gruesome was hiding behind that door, if the wolf having gone to "live in the country" was cover for a reality far more ghastly. If the wolf met a very different end, in Lake City or elsewhere. If the couple with the farm even existed. Sometimes our collective familial memory is like a field riddled with deep holes. You never know when you are going to slip and fall into one.

The grasshoppers are multiplying. Around here they're mainly eastern lubbers, fat and citrus-colored with long legs and bladelike faces. "Lubber" comes from the Old English word "lobre"—lazy—a fitting name for these ambling, flightless pests. I start seeing the lubbers perched like jewels all around my mother's yard, on the narcissi and the birds-of-paradise and the fiddle-leaf fig, nibbling away. They chirp and hop and decimate plant life. The lubbers' wings are too short for flight; they prefer to hunker down on a wide green spade and munch. I start to wonder if we should *do something* about these grasshoppers, but after some research I learn that lubbers are actually quite hard to kill. For starters, they are immune to insecticide. "Let them be," my mother says, waving a hand at the yard. "Don't you know that grasshoppers are good luck?" We're standing outside, surveying the hundred or so grasshoppers that are giving her backyard a distinct aura of pestilence. It is so hot and will only get hotter as we slog deeper into the summer. Petals wilt; steam rises from the streets; every surface is beaded with moisture. *And there will be terrors and great signs from heaven.* My mother, a retired social worker, has many practical skills, but she is also very superstitious. Whenever she passed a slain water bird on the roadside she would wrap it in a blanket and put it in the trunk, take it home, and bury it, a practice that got her kicked out of the neighborhood car pool. She's not had so much as a cold in years and she believes this is because she never goes outside with wet hair. She believes a spider in the doorway means that we will soon have an unexpected visitor. She calls the window in the attic bedroom a witch's window and thinks it is unlucky to enter a house through a back door. When she bought this house, there was a back door off the kitchen, but she had it sealed up, to spare visitors from making that particular mistake. On a walk, I pass a woman in a white tennis dress, armpits dark with sweat, sitting on a park bench. A huge orange grasshopper is perched in her hair like a barrette. "There's something in your hair," I tell her, lunging forward. "Don't touch him!" the woman cries. Her small hands fly up and make a little dome. "He's my only friend."

One night, I fall asleep on the couch in the middle of a Vin Diesel movie, as I find Vin Diesel to be unfathomably comforting. For years I have been accumulating useless facts about him. He has a twin brother. When he moved to LA his first job was in telemarketing. He wrote, produced, directed, and starred in his first two movies; both were selected for Cannes. Vin Diesel started out wanting to be a dramatic actor, an auteur. When the movie ends, I go into the kitchen for a glass of water. As I stand at the sink and fill my glass I get the strange feeling that I'm being watched. I turn to the window and there is a grasshopper, big and yellow as a lemon, pressed to the pane, looking in, its head cocked as though it has just experienced a revelation.

Sinkholes

My mother's house is tilted. This too is not a metaphor. One smoldering afternoon my husband points out a slope in the kitchen. To demonstrate he fills a glass, kneels down, and dribbles water onto the floor. He's still in his running shorts and sneakers, shirtless and tanned and sweat-shined. We watch the water slide down the slope, as though summoned by a force we cannot see. Upon further examination we discover that the living room floor is sloped too, as are the floors in the upstairs bedrooms. Even the front door is a little off center. We wonder if this is a sign that my mother's house is on the verge of collapse. All our adult lives we have been apartment people; houses are an immense and wondrous mystery. So much space. So many things that can go wrong. "Things shift around" is all my mother has to say about these discrepancies. She reminds us that most of Florida is built atop porous limestone, that nearly everything around here is some kind of Ponzi scheme, right down to the earth. The mention of limestone makes me think of sinkholes, hardly a reassuring thought. A few days later, we take our dog to a state park and in the middle of a green field we find a crater circled with yellow temporary fencing. A sign explains that a sinkhole appeared there last summer. At first county officials thought it might be a new spring, a theory that turned out to be false. The hole has continued to grow, widening into a deep and ominous maw. The parks department thinks there might be caverns underneath; they are bringing in geological experts to investigate. We peer through the fencing and down into the crater, at the dark glint of moist earth. Our dog chews the grass, indifferent. When we get home, I google "sinkholes" and read an article titled "Why Sinkholes Are Eating Florida." I read about a man in Tampa who died after a sinkhole opened underneath his house. I do not tell my husband what I learned about that poor man, the horror of being inhaled by the earth while you're watching *Maury* in your living room. I do not tell him that—due to rapid population growth—Florida has been draining its groundwater supply, further destabilizing all that limestone. Or that I have started watching my mother's yard with a new alertness. They say that just before a sinkhole opens you can see the ground tremble.

My mother's house was built in 1902, a white Queen Anne with a redbrick chimney because the original builder was from New York and came south to make his fortune in the celery trade. When my mother bought the house, it was in a state of total disrepair. In the yard the overgrowth was so dense, you couldn't see through the vines to the back of the lot. But it was next door to the Craftsman bungalow my sister—pregnant at the time—and her husband had spent several years rehabilitating. My mother worked on her own renovation for six months and then ran out of steam, so the house remains a project that will never be finished. For example, the wiring is a little strange. Sometimes I'm reading on the couch and all the lights just go dark, as if an invisible hand has come to switch them off.

How did we wind up here, shipwrecked at my mother's house? In Florida, this is a question I ask myself every day.

At the start of the year, we came down to help care for my father, who was dying for some time and is now dead. In the aftermath, my husband and I had planned to return to our lives, but then the pandemic happened and we couldn't go anywhere. My husband used to be a visiting professor in a history department at a university in upstate New York, but during the pandemic the department's budget was slashed and they no longer had use for visitors of any kind. My husband believes that if he wants to get another job he must first finish his book on pilgrimages. Meanwhile, I chip away at ghostwriting thrillers. So far this year has felt like living under a giant blanket, out of view of the wider world, but underneath that blanket exists a whole universe of memory and association and experience. I am never alone. Under the blanket I have, to my absolute horror, all my former selves for company.

In upstate New York, we lived in university housing, so now we have nothing to reclaim. "Who knows what's out there anyway," my sister tells me when I bemoan our current situation. "Better to stay close to home, where you're safe." My sister is an adjuster for an insurance company and likes to think that she has a keen sense of risk management. I remind her that a very strange energy is circulating in the atmosphere down here. For one thing, the local newspaper is filled with articles about missing persons. Nextdoor is teeming with pleas to call with any information about people who have vanished. I have never seen so many photos of faces crying out from the abyss. We're sitting in lounge chairs in her backyard, watching my niece play a game where she can talk to every blade of grass and every blade of grass can talk back. My niece is four and in possession of a boundless and deranged imagination. She seems to believe, for example, that she has acquired a pet ghost. "You've been away your whole life. What's wrong with just staying here, where you're needed?" my sister replies, crossing her sun-bronzed arms. She has never left Florida or expressed any desire to be elsewhere. This is one of the many differences between us. Another difference: she also got sick during the pandemic but insists that she feels exactly the same, as though she thinks I haven't noticed that her eye color has changed from a maritime blue-green to a feline green-gold. Trauma can alter us in the most unexpected ways. I left Florida when I was twenty-two and now I'm thirty-six. "Half a life," I correct her.

· · ·

My mother's house has an attic bedroom with a pitched roof and a single porthole window that looks out onto the street. The walls are lined with Bankers Boxes and plastic bins. These boxes contain things like rag dolls with missing eyes and tablecloths permanently marred with mustard stains because my mother does not believe in throwing anything away. In her opinion, failures of foresight are the worst kind. An antique davenport faces the porthole window. The desk is burr walnut, with three drawers on either side, small brass lion heads for pulls. I place a stool in front of the desk. I sit down. The legs are uneven, so I sway a little in the attic, as though I really am at sea. On some nights, I hear sirens for hours. Something is broken, and the alarm won't stop sounding. My half brother lives in the Panhandle, where he runs an ecotour outfit; recently a group of men in camo booked one of his tours, in hopes of finding a remote island where they could establish a camp. *You don't really believe in all that global warming nonsense, do you?* one of the men asked my half brother. *Don't you know that heat and floods come in cycles? It's been that way since biblical times. Ever heard of Noah?* I decide that I will use this attic room for ghostwriting, yes, but also to think about other things. Like what I want from Florida and what Florida wants from me. How this place got inside us and moved all the parts around and how we have done the same in return. If we should believe what we hear in our dreams. What vows of silence should be kept forever and which ones must be broken.

. . .

In the next Ask Ava column, a man writes in about his mother, who has recently gone missing. She had been living with her son in a small guest room off the kitchen. She used to spend her time watching telenovelas and chatting with friends on the phone, but during the pandemic she started using MIND'S EYE. She would crawl into bed and put the white headset on and stay like that for hours, her body inert but her mind rollicking. The letter writer's mother stopped tracking the intricate plots of the telenovelas; she stopped calling her friends. He thought that perhaps he might need to stage an intervention, but then one day he opened the door to her bedroom and found that she was gone. Everything else in her room appeared to be normal. Apart from his mother, the white headset was the only thing that was missing. She was not in the house or in the backyard or on their street. She is retired; she does not drive. He called all her friends. He called the police, who seemed overwhelmed, indifferent. *Do you have any idea how many reports we're getting a day? Before we know it, we're going to have more missing people than found ones.* He searched all the places she might have gone; he erected signs; he posted on Nextdoor. He has been tempted to borrow a neighbor's MIND'S EYE, to try to investigate whatever kind of life his mother was leading in there—but he can't bring himself to do it. ELECTRA gives him a queasy feeling. What if the device is causing something inside the users to misfire, like how subliminal messages in music can warp pathways in the brain? *Go where you need to be, they tell us, but how can I trust a tech company to know what that is?* he writes. *Also, if I can't find her, or if she doesn't want to be found, can you advise on the ethics of renting out her bedroom?*

The thing about holes, Ava says in her reply, *is that you can't force them to close.*

My mother was raised in Tennessee and used to own a place there, a small cabin in Pulaski on a man-made lake filled with snakes. Her father built the cabin with his very own hands, though she was the only one in her family who ever expressed any interest in residing there, perhaps because of the persistent copperhead infestations or because all the neighbors look like they could be members of a far-right militia. Two years ago—before the pandemic struck and left our world forever changed—my mother announced to me and my sister that she had been diagnosed with advanced pancreatic cancer. She wanted to sell her house in Florida and return to the cabin in Tennessee, because the lakeside community reminded her of childhood. My mother maintains that childhood was the happiest time in her life. "These are my people," she kept insisting, "even if half of them are Church of Christ and crazy as hell." At her request, my sister and I traveled to Pulaski to visit her at the cabin. My sister rarely travels and checked a massive suitcase even though we were only staying the weekend; at baggage claim it took both of us to roll it off the conveyor belt. In Pulaski, we met Mr. Blessing, ex-military and head of the Lakeside Community Association. The skin on his face looked like it had been pulled back a little too tight. His living room smelled of mothballs and artificial cinnamon, the windows blocked by towers of cardboard boxes. Mr. Blessing seemed to spend most of his time standing on his back deck with tactical binoculars, surveying the surrounding lots for copperheads. When he spotted one, he would give the coordinates to his second-in-command, Mr. Folks, also ex-military, who would then run over to the location and dispatch the snake with a rifle. "These are my people," my mother kept saying. "Just wait until you post a yard sign for the next Democratic presidential candidate," my sister and I countered. "We'll see if they're still your people then." At the cabin, my sister and I shared a bed. We stayed up late, talking strategy in a humid hush. We wondered if our mother was, in the face of her diagnosis, having a nervous collapse. How else to explain her sudden desire to live under the auspices of Mr. Blessing and Mr. Folks? I would wake in the middle of the night and find my sister curled into a fetal position and weeping into her pillow. I would stroke her hair—hazelnut brown and silky straight—but this gesture of care only made her cry harder. To calm myself I thought about the copperheads. Didn't Mr. Blessing know that the snakes were migrating north because of climate change? That it was our own stupid fault that they kept showing up where they weren't supposed to be? I've read that snakes will have migrated to northern Canada by 2050. I wonder if this means there will be fewer snakes in Florida, or if different kinds will start appearing in different places. At the moment, there are approximately 150,000 Burmese pythons in the Everglades. On our last night at the cabin, our mother sat us down and confessed that she did not have advanced pancreatic cancer after all. As it turned out, the doctor's office had confused her ultrasound images with another patient's. She didn't tell us right away, because, well, she had been feeling a little jealous of all the attention our father— recently diagnosed with a terminal lung condition—was getting now that he was dying. Our mother was our father's second wife. The first marriage produced my half brother— fifteen years older, more like an uncle really—the second, my sister and me. Our parents divorced a decade ago, after a marriage so long and hostile it was possible for my mother to believe that our concern for our dying father was misplaced, that whatever he was going through was nothing compared with her own suffering, even if she did not happen to be suffering from advanced pancreatic cancer specifically. In the cabin, my sister went red and quaking. She held a ruffled decorative pillow so tightly that I thought her knuckles were going to split through her skin. Her jaw turned to stone. Her temples pulsed. She began to sweat profusely. Blood dripped from her right nostril. She stood up and clutched the pillow to her stomach and screamed. Eventually she stormed out of the cabin and insisted on spending the night in our rental car. I went outside to check on her at three in the morning and found her reclined in the passenger seat, the ruffled pillow positioned over her face.

After my mother found a copperhead coiled in her bathtub she decided that maybe she didn't want to live in Pulaski after all. She took her house in Florida off the market and sold the cabin to Mr. Blessing, who was looking to expand his holdings around the lake. "It's just as well," my mother said at the time. After all, the only place to eat near the cabin was a café run by a cult, though they did make the most delicious cakes.

When our mother first met our father he had incredible ESP. He could predict the weather. He could sense things before they happened. He dreamed things that later became real. Then one day he fell down the stairs and broke his shoulder. After that, he never had another premonition again. For a long time there was a portal and then, one day, it closed. This is perhaps the nicest story our mother has ever told us about him.

My husband and I were in Florida for two weeks before my father died. This happened back in February. By then we knew his death was coming, but it was not supposed to happen so soon. We were supposed to spend months watching old westerns and heating soups and tapping chalky pills into his palm, with me staying put in Florida and my husband flying back and forth to teach his classes. That had been the whole point of us coming down here, to accompany my father through the twilight. I had steeled myself for John Wayne westerns, since John Wayne was my father's favorite movie star. He used to keep a life-size cardboard cutout— cowboy hat shadowing the actor's face, gun drawn—in his home office. My father dreamed of being lawless. Because he had a lung condition his death would come by drowning. We wanted him to see our faces when he stared up through the sheen of the water. To know that we were there.

One afternoon he went into the hospital because he was having trouble breathing. That day the sky was blue, the air light and cool. Our half brother drove down from the Panhandle to join me and my sister. The three of us took turns spending the night in my father's room, and on the third night my sister called at two in the morning to tell us that he had sprung from his bed and, in a surprising show of strength, torn all the IVs from his arms. He ripped away his hospital gown too and stood before her—naked and trembling in the sallow light, tall as ever but newly emaciated, blood bubbling from his veins—and pleaded with her to take him home. Pleaded like a child who wants one more turn at a ride. Who is not yet ready for the obliterating overness. "What do I do?" she said to us on the phone. "What do I do?" My sister bears a strong resemblance to our father. She got the height, the olive skin, the hawkish eyes, the long flat feet. When our

LAURA VAN DEN BERG

father stood before her, naked and disoriented and dripping blood, I wonder if it felt like her own death foretold.

I don't remember the night-soaked drive to the hospital. I just remember being delivered into a tremendous fluorescent brightness. Afterlife. Aftermath. I remember having to hand my bag over to a security guard to be searched. I remember that there were some things the security guard said I could not take inside and I said, "Keep them." I remember an elevator, white hallway after white hallway, blade-sharp corners. By the time my brother and I arrived our father was unconscious. A pair of nurses had managed to wrestle him into a fresh hospital gown and back under the blood-spotted sheets. My father did not want to get back into that bed, because he knew he would never get out. He knew that if he did not make a break for it, the tan walls and the hissing machines would be the last things he would see on this earth— and he was right. His body had gone mad with infection, his blood septic. Dead by morning. After he died, his skin was not as cold as I had thought it would be. Cool, but not cold. I held his left shoulder, the one he shattered all those years ago, the fracture in the body that caused the fracture in consciousness. He still looked like himself, but he did not smell like himself. He smelled like metal and chemicals, with a sour funk hovering underneath. In the immediate aftermath, smell was the clearest evidence that a fundamental change had occurred. I had never cried before like I did in that room. I beat my fists against my chest and wailed, snotty and gasping and woolly headed. Like an exorcism except the demon was getting in instead of being cast out. Samuel Beckett once described tears as "liquefied brain," and that was just how I felt; everything inside me was being melted down into one trembling pool. These days I am relieved that at least my father did not have to endure the pandemic and its bewildering afterlife. My sister still won't admit that her eyes are now a different color; when she's upset the gold flecks in her irises shimmer, catch the light. She downplays the fact that, each time she uses MIND'S EYE, our father appears and tells her *There is something I want you to do* before fading into the air like a vanishing hologram. "Are you sure you're not thinking the word 'dad'?" I asked her once, but she told me no, that he just comes, though who is to say what might be occurring in the underbrush of her thoughts. "I wouldn't mind seeing him," she said, "if he didn't make so many demands." My sister's favorite MIND'S EYE meditation invites her into a lush and fragrant English garden. At the end of the garden path, she sits down on a stone bench and feels the warmth of the sun on her face, and this is where our father finds her. *There is something I want you to do.* My sister was always his favorite child.

At the funeral, our half brother told a story about our dad taking him on a cruise. When the time came to dock for an excursion, a long line formed to board the motorboats that would ferry the passengers to land. Our father, who hated lines, somehow talked a crew member into letting him use an inflatable life raft instead. After he lowered the raft into the water, he dove over the ship railing with the paddles and then ordered his son to jump. At the service, my brother paused to say that this happened a long time ago, when there were looser safety regulations, and also that this vessel was much smaller than the cruise ships of today. Still, the drop was steep and he was afraid. Finally he hurled himself over the edge—fists clenched, eyes shut tight—and our father caught him in his arms. Slung him around like a baby. At the end of the service, we played a recording of a bugler performing taps, in honor of our father's (very brief) military service. Like dutiful soldiers, we followed the orders even if we could no longer recall exactly where they had come from. Our father had a gift for convincing people to follow him into the wilderness, a quality that made him both dangerous and magical. He spent the whole of his adult life in Florida and that is how I have come to think of this place too, as equal parts danger and magic. I think this is what my half brother's story must have been intended to demonstrate at the funeral, that hell-heaven state.

"There were always so many other women," my mother sometimes tells me when she's had a little too much to drink. For whatever reason, she does not recall their names or what they looked like; she only identifies them by what they did for a living. "Legal secretaries, judicial assistants, manicurists, hairdressers . . ."

After my father died, I started reading the newspaper classifieds, to see if there were any wolves for sale, but these days there are no ads for animals in the local paper and even fewer for jobs. Frankie's Cleaners is seeking a presser. *No experience needed. Will train.* I find a notice of public sale for OFF THE CHAIN TOWING. An estate sale on Feather Lane. *Collectibles, antiques, some tools, Persian rugs, dining room set 8 chairs, French canopy bed with matching dresser, artificial plants.* Someone is selling a generator, a two-way radio, a sump pump, and fifteen sandbags. I can only imagine this person has plans to move to higher ground. Someone is selling a collection of antique handheld mirrors. Someone is seeking private security for a family compound. Pay commensurate with experience. A medium in Cassadaga is offering her services to anyone seeking a post-pandemic missing person. A man has taken out an ad to advocate for himself as a write-in candidate for the next gubernatorial election. His qualifications include having lived "off the grid" for the last decade on seventeen dollars a month. Interested parties can mail two stamps to an address in Palatka for further information. A family is seeking information about the hit-and-run driver who killed their son. The ad describes the following: A motorcycle collided with a vehicle in which their son was a passenger. Unharmed, the son rushed into the road to help the motorcyclist, who was gravely injured, only to be struck and killed by a different driver who then fled the scene. The ad includes a black-and-white composite sketch of the suspect, a middle-aged man with sagging jowls and a limp bowl cut. The ad concedes that eyewitnesses have conflicting descriptions, so the sketch might not be entirely accurate. I assume this must have been a recent death, but then I read that their son was killed nine years ago. The family has been looking for the driver ever since.

On Sundays, my sister and I take my niece to visit the cemetery where our father is buried. The cemetery is very old, rumored to be haunted. Visitors have reported seeing a blond woman in dripping wet clothes leaning against a tree and weeping. At the cemetery, we stick to the charming stories: "Did you know that when your grandfather was in the military, he kept a hamster illegally in his barracks and exercised it on a Victrola?" We leave out ones like "Did you know that your grandfather once screamed at your grandmother so loudly a window broke, or that he once locked your uncle in a closet when he was a little boy, so he could have sex with a woman who was not his wife? That is how your grandfather ended up in his first D-I-V-O-R-C-E." The journey to the cemetery involves an accursed interstate known as I-4, which runs from Tampa to Daytona Beach. On I-4, we pass lakes that look like giant mirrors, the way they cradle the reflections of the clouds in the water. The "I-4 corridor" is famous for having the highest percentage of so-called undecided voters, as opposed to the solid blocks of red and blue found elsewhere. Also, there is the matter of the Field of the Dead. In the late 1800s, the St. Joseph's Catholic Colony, made up of German immigrants who had bought several hundred acres from a real estate tycoon, was devastated by yellow fever. The dead were buried in mass graves; the living fled. Many decades later, the Field of the Dead was sold to the county. Later still, when public officials started snatching up land for highway construction, the Field of the Dead was sold to the state. The graves were supposed to be relocated but ended up just being paved over. Now this stretch of I-4 is unusually prone to fatal car accidents. Dropped phone signals. Blasts of static on the radios. Windows that go as cold as ice.

One afternoon my niece took me by the hand and led me to her bedroom window. She told me she wanted to show me her pet ghost. I blame the arrival of this pet ghost on the fact that her parents won't let her have so much as a goldfish. *I'm busy day and night*, I've heard my sister say. *I'm exhausted. I'm overwhelmed. I'll kill a goldfish without even meaning to.* My niece pointed at the grass outside and asked if I could see her pet ghost. "Does your pet ghost have a name?" I replied, and she told me that ghosts don't have names. Next I asked what her pet ghost does out there all day and she said her pet ghost spends most of its time eating dirt in the backyard.

. . .

I-4 is also home to the WORLD'S 2ND LARGEST CONFED-
ERATE FLAG, which looms over the I-75 and I-4 intersection
in Tampa. This fifty-by-thirty-foot monstrosity was recently
removed by the Tampa chapter of the Sons of Confederate Veterans because people kept setting the flag on fire. If
the flag ever returns I hope a massive sinkhole immediately
opens beneath it. My mother says that groups like the Sons
of Confederate Veterans will soon become extinct, that their
members are all old and dying out, but when I look up this
chapter online I see young white men—college age or even
younger—in the photos. They all look to be the same type of
white: blondish, sweaty, pink. Whiteness as a sickness that is
passed on and on. On the Facebook page for the Sons of Confederate Veterans, I find a photo of a man in a mullet and a
Guns N' Roses T-shirt posing in the flag's giant shadow, legs
spread and biceps flexed. I find another of a young girl wearing a replica of a Confederate uniform and playing a flute,
elbows flared out, eyes shut tight in apparent concentration.

I happen to think all of I-4 is cursed and not just the part
occupying the Field of the Dead. The interstate has been under construction for years and years—for the whole of my
life, in fact. In some areas, the roadsides are so crowded with
machines and workers in hard hats that it feels like you're
driving on a concrete tightrope. The official name for this

hellscape is the Ultimate Improvement Project. Because of all this "improvement," exits are always changing; sometimes they disappear altogether. Today my sister and I are nearing the one for the cemetery and *poof*—the exit is gone. There is just a small crater in the black asphalt, as if the exit itself might have been taken by a sinkhole, though we know better. Has the exit for the cemetery just been closed temporarily? Is it ever coming back? We look and look for signs.

After the pandemic, I wondered where *my* evidence of physical trauma lived, given that I had the fever too and, unlike my sister, my eyes are the same color as they were before. In the shower one morning I notice that my belly button has been transformed from an outie to an innie. A perfect concave circle, as though something inside me has simply collapsed. I stick my finger in there, swirl around some water and soap. I get out of the shower and rush downstairs, leaving a trail of watery footprints. I find my husband in the kitchen, reading some tome on pilgrimages and eating a sliced orange; each time he sinks his teeth into a glistening wedge, juice rains down onto the pages. "Those at sea cannot be counted among either the living or the dead," he says, pressing a fingertip to the text. "Look!" I point at my belly button. His head snaps up from the book, black eyebrows raised. "Notice anything?" I ask, and when he doesn't reply I tell him to look carefully at my belly button. He sets the tome down and gazes at my stomach for a minute and then confesses, "Men don't notice belly buttons. They just notice what's above and below." I inform him that he would've made a lousy detective, and head back upstairs. In the bathroom mirror, I bend and stretch my torso, marvel at this transformation in the landscape of my body, this evidence of a change occurring from the inside out.

Fields

One end of my mother's street runs into a square field. On the opposite side of the field, traffic churns on a busy road. I have come to think of this field as a kind of town square; all manner of stories unfold in the parched green center. On some nights people drive their cars across the field and park along the edges. The drivers switch on their headlights and spotlight children kicking a soccer ball across the illuminated grass. On Tuesday mornings, a lone man plays golf out there, with a single tee that he periodically uproots and moves from one spot to the next. Anhingas and herons scavenge the field for insects and worms after summer storms. Once, I saw a man pedal a bicycle into the center of the field. He dismounted the bike, hurled it to the ground, and left it there. "Fuck this thing," he cried out. "I'll take the bus." The east side of the field is sheltered by a stand of elm trees; feral cats sleep off the afternoon steam in the shade. On the weekends, a man named Mr. Heaven drives his red truck into the field and sells damp bags of boiled peanuts from the bed. Last week, the police attempted to apprehend a murder suspect at the local Laundromat. He ran across the busy road and into the field, where a police officer shot him in the thigh and he collapsed. No rain for two days after, so the grass stayed dark with blood. I've seen a couple staggering through virtual worlds in the same white MIND'S EYE headsets that my sister uses, at times drifting dangerously close to traffic. My mother was the only one in our household who tried the headset the ELECTRA representatives delivered. She used it exactly once and then boxed it up in the attic room. She had selected a meditation by the ocean. Before she knew it, the water was shoulder high and the waves were breaking against her face. "Go where I need to be?" she said. "No thanks." For days she claimed to still be able to taste the salt in her mouth.

Once, I saw a woman march out into the center of the field, press her hands over her ears, bend at the waist, and scream. It was the most anguished sound I have ever heard emerge from another human being, and it went on and on like an aria. People on the sidewalk stopped. Cars stopped. I stopped. The feral cats shot up from the shade and scattered. The woman walking in front of me, a cell phone in one hand and a purple umbrella in the other, held the speaker out toward the field, so the other person could hear what was going on. "If she's not careful," the woman said, twirling her purple umbrella, "she is going to wake the dead."

I read a story in the local paper about a man who practiced his knife-throwing skills in the field. He used an elm for target practice. "Shame on him," my mother says when I tell her. "Doesn't he know that trees can communicate with one another? That they can experience pain?" During one attempt the man missed the trunk and hurled the knife deep into the trees. Before he could cross the field and retrieve his weapon, a man in a white tank top and green cargo shorts emerged from the trees with a black knife handle jutting out of his left shoulder. The knife thrower raced over to his victim. He called 911. He told the stabbed man that he might want to lie down. The stabbed man was strangely calm, even though blood was spraying from the wound. Probably he was in shock. "How about that aim," he kept saying. "How about it." He chattered away until the paramedics arrived and loaded him onto a stretcher. Apparently the man had come to tend to the community garden, a rectangular plot bordered by a wire fence. This garden appears to have been abandoned by its community, with desiccated stalks slumped over in stone-dry beds, though perhaps the stabbed man had arrived to address this neglect. He was walking away from the garden when the knife sank into his shoulder. The force of the attack shoved him ass-first onto the ground. When he looked down the steel blade had disappeared into his body and blood was rising through his tank top. "I couldn't see anyone around," he told the local newspaper from his hospital bed. "At first I thought I'd been stabbed by a ghost."

My mother's stories could fill a field. Some nights, we sit out on the front porch and she says that there is something she wants to tell me about my father's life, something she has never shared before. Something she'll only tell me now that he's gone.

"Are you sure I haven't heard this one already?" I'll ask her.

"Positive," she'll say.

Of course, I know better, because it's the same two stories over and over.

Here is the first:

"Your father's mother did not actually die of a heart attack. Well, at least that's not the whole story. Your grandfather pushed her down a flight of stairs. And then she had a heart attack and then she died. Did you know he waited hours before he called for an ambulance? Did you know that she spent her whole life in misery? I had to clean out her bedroom and I found all these sad little notes stuffed into the backs of drawers and in her shoes and under the mattress. All of them were written on tiny scraps of paper, on cocktail napkins and receipts, even though she had exquisite stationery."

This is my mother's way of telling me that violence runs in my father's family.

Here is the second:

"The day we got back from our honeymoon, your father and me, the phone rang. I picked up and it was this woman. Saying she was pregnant and my new husband was the father. I asked her how far along and she said twelve weeks. As you know, your father and I dated for six months before we married. So you can do the math. Your father denied everything. He yanked the phone away from me and called her a liar and an extortionist. Even though I never heard her ask for money."

"Do you know what ever happened to her?" I always ask my mother. "If she got an abortion or if she had the baby?"

"Babies," my mother clarifies. On the phone, the woman had told her that she was pregnant with twins.

At this point, silence falls like a curtain. Not a pause, but the kind of silence that stretches on and on, cavernous and consuming. A pit we could both fall into, never to be seen again. On my end of the silence, I imagine the twins alive and out in the world. What are they like? If I passed them on the street, would there be a shiver of recognition? All these different possibilities. The endless ways a life can fork.

"I always believed her," my mother says.

At the Institute, I sometimes imagined that my own self had been split, and that these two halves were wrestling around inside me. One twin wanted to live and the other wanted to die. They took turns leg sweeping and choke holding, joint locking and striking and grappling around in the muck. How did the twin who wanted to live prevail? Even today I can't say for sure. The human mind is a great thicket of mystery. So much remains unknown. And yet we are expected—in fact, required—to live our lives alongside this inscrutable entity that might, at any moment, turn on us.

· · ·

On the edge of the field, a man sets up a red tent stocked with illegal Fourth of July fireworks. Also: books. As it turns out, the tent owner is a writer. He has authored three "pararescue thrillers" featuring one John Paxton, a decorated air force sergeant. These books have plots like the thrillers I ghostwrite, with their unambiguous villains and heroes. Anyone who buys a John Paxton thriller gets 15 percent off on the skyrockets, 25 percent off on the torpedoes. To the left of the field, just beyond the elm trees and the community garden, is a bail bonds outfit called Quick Release. To the right is a bar called Manikins. One morning I'm walking the dog when I see the screaming woman stagger out of Manikins and in the direction of the field. She's dressed in pink shorts and a red T-shirt and filthy white sneakers. Sobbing so hard she's doubled over, her shoulders quaking. When she reaches the field, she sinks onto the ground. She sits with her legs crossed and her face in her hands, still sobbing. On the other side of the field, the fireworks tent is just starting to open. I watch the owner trot across the scorched grass with a paperback tucked under his arm. He leaves the book on the ground, a safe distance from the wailing woman. Maybe she'll think her own problems aren't so dire after she reads about John Paxton having to escape from an underground bunker or from a fighter jet nose-diving toward the earth.

Bankers Financial Corporation, the largest bail insurer in the country, is located in Florida. Bankers is well known for providing coverage against natural disasters, but it also maintains Bankers Surety, a bail bonds insurance company. In this twisted ecosystem, the bail bondsmen wield unchecked power. They can extort their clients with punishing fees, arrest them without cause, subject them to curfews and ankle monitors. True to the Floridian spirit, these outfits know how to exploit vulnerability and desperation. Quick Release is one of many bail bonds offices that line this particular stretch of road. All of them look like humble storefronts, square concrete boxes with little neon signs curled in the windows, but they are debt traps, backed by massive companies. They stake themselves around the jails and bars like spiders stringing up webs.

Before I was institutionalized, I went on a bender that lasted for three weeks. I was nineteen and, quite literally, falling-down drunk, my knees and shins so purpled with bruises it looked like someone had been beating me. By then I had scraped through high school and was enrolled in night classes at a local college, though I rarely went. All I can say about this period of time is that I felt like I had a head full of bees and I wanted to kill the hive. One summer morning I ran away on a Greyhound bus to stay with a woman in Tallahassee. Her name was Rita and we'd met at a nightclub in Orlando some weeks prior. I must have complained about home, because she gave me her information and told me I could come stay with her whenever I wanted. True to her word, she did not seem alarmed when I turned up at her door. She was in her thirties and at the nightclub she had kept calling me *sweetheart*. On the bus I had fantasized about Rita becoming my mother. She had feathered blond hair and a tattoo of a sword on the back of her neck. She lived in an apartment near Florida State, though she had no connection to the university. I remember very little about the place itself or the surrounding area. We drank when we got up in the morning. We kept the blinds closed. We smoked cigarettes, we watched *Mister Ed* reruns, we ate microwavable cups of mac and cheese, we had dance parties. Rita let me sleep in her bed, a mattress on the floor with a single pillow covered by a thin hunter green duvet. The duvet was soft and smelled of menthol cigarettes. A few other details live in sharper relief: the Pepto-pink bathroom, the shallow white tub. We vomited so much we were always out of toilet paper, tissues, clean towels. I can see my younger self crouched like a feral animal under the showerhead as water gushed down. Right on the edge of the wilderness. One night I passed out on Rita's couch and woke to find a strange man kneeling beside me with his hand up my shirt. "Go back to sleep," he whispered, and I did. *What does it matter?* I thought at the time. Later I would learn this was Rita's boyfriend (until then I had not been aware that she had one). One night I woke up to find a large, slobbery bulldog licking vomit off my face and chest (I had, apparently, thrown up on myself in the middle of the night). Later I would learn that the bulldog, T-Rex, belonged to Rita's boyfriend (until then I had not been aware that he had one). I can't remember ever seeing the boyfriend or the dog come or go from the apartment. It was like they lived in a closet and just materialized in the dead of night.

Drinking was a portal. It delivered me into these other worlds, all of them twisted and troubled, but at least the hive in my head hummed at a lower pitch.

One strange thing about Rita's apartment was the unexplained disappearances. One minute my lighter was on her coffee table; the next it was nowhere to be found. A pink ankle sock vanished into the recesses of her bedroom, never to be seen again. I assumed I had forfeited the ability to keep track of the tangible world, but Rita's boyfriend often complained about the things that had been lost to the apartment: a wallet, two TV remotes, two phone chargers, a pair of white tube socks, a glass pipe. One night, he sat next to me on the couch and explained that the apartment was afflicted. *With what?* I asked. *This place is like the Bermuda Triangle,* he replied. *It just sucks things up like a big hungry mouth.* He said he was a scholar of paranormal events and specialized in unexplained vanishings.

This happened in the early 2000s. I had a flip phone, a MySpace, an AIM handle. My parents had no idea where

I had gone. Addicts are not known for being considerate, and indeed I had not been courteous enough to leave a note. My sister—sixteen at the time—took to watching *Unsolved Mysteries* reruns for hours on end. After seeing the episode on Tammy Lynn Leppert, who disappeared from Cocoa Beach at eighteen, she became convinced that I had been abducted by a madman. Leppert was an aspiring actress; shortly before her disappearance she snagged a minor role in *Scarface*. In the scene, she wears a blue bikini and leans into a convertible to distract the lookout driver while Angel and Tony Montana are held captive in a Miami Beach hotel. In a shower stall, a cartel leader dismembers Angel with a chain saw as Tony waits for his turn, except by then Leppert's character has moved along and the lookout drivers realize, at long last, that something is amiss, and rush the hotel room with guns blazing. Reportedly Tammy Lynn Leppert became so panicked at the sight of fake blood that she would start hyperventilating and had to be removed from the set. The FBI's best guess is that Leppert was the victim of the serial killer Christopher Wilder, who was active in Florida at the time and who lured women into his RV by offering to photograph them for magazines. "After I heard about Tammy Lynn Leppert, I was sure you were never coming back," my sister told me later. "I started to picture a life in which I had no sister." She shared these memories with me during a road trip through the coastal wilderness of the Panhandle. She held the steering wheel so tight I thought she might lose circulation in her fingers. She told me that a part of her childhood had been stolen, that while I was drinking my heart out in Tallahassee she was losing something—a lightness, an innocence—that she would never recover. In the end, my parents found me after Rita and her boyfriend and T-Rex dumped me outside an ER in north Florida to be treated for alcohol poisoning. "We've lost you," my father said when he parted the white curtain and saw me in the hospital bed, even though I had, technically speaking, just been found.

Throughout his life, the serial killer Christopher Wilder told people that he nearly died in a childhood drowning accident, and when he came out of the water he was not the same. He emerged with a mind that trembled with glistening, murderous thoughts. After FBI profilers interviewed his family, however, they determined the drowning story was likely an invention. Christopher Wilder's family claimed that he was terrified of bodies of water as a child, refused to go near them.

On the way home from Tallahassee my hive-killing thoughts compelled me to open the passenger door and hurl myself onto the highway. We were stuck in rush hour traffic, and my father wasn't doing more than twenty, so I just rolled out into the emergency lane. Stood up and looked around, aching and confused. "You have ten seconds to get back in this car," my father shouted through an open window. I obeyed. I remember little about the rest of the drive beyond the insistent throbbing in the back of my head and the thunder of my father's voice. *It is an insult to your mother and me, all these attempts to destroy yourself. Don't you know that your grandparents had to survive war? Famine?* At home, I hugged my mother and my sister. I told them I loved them and that I was sorry. I told them I was very tired and needed to sleep. Then I went upstairs and took everything in the medicine cabinet and then I woke up in a hospital with tubes burrowed in my body and an unholy burning in my stomach and then I was transferred to the Institute. I was allowed to call home on Sundays, but my sister refused to talk to me. If she answered she would just pass the phone to our parents. Later I would learn that she had been the one to find me, unconscious in bed, barely breathing.

In the ER, a voice asked, "Do you know where you are?" I only knew I was trapped inside a great pandemonium. A horrific brightness. Even these days I am, at times, surprised to find myself unsure of my whereabouts. For example, I thought that I was pretty well acquainted with the world I lived in, but then the pandemic happened and that world transformed into something else.

After I left the Institute, I got sober and stayed that way. By then I only knew one thing for sure and it was that I never wanted to see the inside of a hospital again. I went back to school. I went to AA and got a sponsor, a middle-aged Pentecostal woman who wore long denim dresses and sometimes called me in the middle of the night to discuss divine healing or pure units of consciousness or the fates of her three daughters. She had lost custody of her girls and longed to get them back. When she got sober, she decided to get baptized as Pentecostal in part because the church forbade alcohol. Once, I asked her if it was true that she could no longer wear pants and she told me that having to wear these dumb dresses was a small price to pay for the salvation of sobriety. *God has put his faith in me and every time I even think about taking a drink I am telling God to go fuck himself.* Eventually the Pentecostal sponsor stopped coming to meetings and I got a new sponsor, an ex-marine with a massive tattoo of a bald eagle, frozen in flight, on his chest. One day the ex-marine found me standing outside on a break. I had been staring directly into the sun, just to see what would happen, when I felt a rough hand on my shoulder and a voice telling me, "You know what you do with those feelings, bruh? You bury that shit. You bury that shit so deep you couldn't find it again if you tried." The ex-marine called everyone *bruh*, regardless of gender, and his advice sounded like a path I could follow, so I took it. I got to digging. I buried my feelings alive and scrubbed the dirt from my hands. In a couple years I would be leaving Florida for that doctoral program in Boston, an event I could not have fathomed when I was standing out in the blistering sunshine and listening to the ex-marine. Only later would I understand that the ex-marine had left out a crucial detail: that one day those feelings might dig their way out and come looking for you.

Of course, all this is behind me now.

In the rearview. That was a saying my father used when he did not want to revisit events that belonged to the past.

Except sometimes it isn't.

Except sometimes those feelings track me down with the swift expertise of a hit squad.

All those years ago I decided I wanted to live, but what exactly have I been doing with that life I chose to save?

This is one reason why I get so frustrated with filling in the famous author's plots. All these feelings roiling around inside me—sometimes I wish I had a story to put them in.

My sister's rage could fill a field. I am certain she has never forgiven me for leaving Florida to become a "student of literature," whatever that means. She is enraged with our mother, who she feels owes us both—but her in particular—an unpayable debt. This is because our mother, the retired social worker, spent so many hours on the job, engrossed in the problems of other families. I thought motherhood might soften my sister's old hurts, but from what I can tell parenthood has only torn open her childhood wounds. My sister has everything she claims to want—a family, a home, a well-paying job—and still there is a void. She used to be enraged with our father but doesn't see the point now that he's dead. In fact, I have never seen my sister forgive someone so easily. Now she only talks about what she loved about him, what she misses, as though nonexistence has wiped his ledger clean. *All you have to do to be forgiven by my sister*, I joke with my husband, *is to die*. She is often enraged at her own husband, for not better understanding the nature of her rage or why she must spend so many hours in that MIND'S EYE headset, swimming around in virtual worlds. We both got sick during the pandemic, but my sister got much sicker, with a fever that would not stop spiking. Fourteen days beet-faced and shedding sweat, as though all that rage was rising to the surface. Now when I ask her about the curious new color of her eyes or what she thinks our father is talking about when he appears in the English garden, she tells me she is tired of discussing things that have already happened, even though *she* is the one who wants to talk about the past—the distant past—all the time. Whenever I walk out her door it's like she's sixteen again and I am boarding that Greyhound bus and vanishing into some gruesome ether. The problem, I have decided, with people who never leave home is that they are never forced to become someone else. After the *Unsolved Mysteries* episode aired, a woman in Des Moines called the tip line and said she'd just seen Tammy Lynn Leppert at the grocery store, alive and well. She'd been waiting in line behind her, so she had gotten a good look. The woman reported that Tammy Lynn was not holding a basket or pushing a cart. She had just one item tucked under her slender arm: a large tub of vanilla yogurt.

Why do people tell stories? Here are some reasons I have come up with:

People tell stories to will lies into truth.

People tell stories to bend truth into lies.

People tell stories to carve for themselves a legible shape out of an inexplicable existence.

People tell stories to atone for what they have failed to do in life.

I don't regard my work as a ghost as storytelling, by the way. The novels I ghostwrite are more like a mirage: they appear to be stories, but they are not. They are not stories, because there is no deeper impetus.

I long to write a story with a deeper impetus.

· · ·

One Saturday, I walk out into the field and buy some boiled peanuts from Mr. Heaven. "Thank you, Mr. Heaven," I say when he hands me the wet, swollen bag. He's wearing jeans and a white T-shirt and a black-and-turquoise Marlins cap. I watch Mr. Heaven sit down on a plastic crate and open a paperback, a thriller by the famous author. I glance at the title and see that it's one I ghostwrote. "What do you think of that book?" I ask Mr. Heaven. "Pure trash," he says without looking up, "but I sure can't stop turning the pages."

Night Shift

My brother-in-law works at a factory on the edge of town. There it is his job to catch other people's mistakes. A mistake is never his mistake unless he fails to catch it. So long as he catches the mistakes they will always belong to someone else. The mistake-makers are assigned to the day shift, so he never has to interact with them. My brother-in-law has admitted that the anonymity makes his job much easier, as it would be difficult to inflict suffering on a person you had to face daily, an outlook that accounts for many things about our sad era, including the current state of the internet. The factory is close to the municipal airport. In the parking lot the black asphalt trembles whenever planes soar overhead. My brother-in-law works the night shift, so he arrives at the factory at six in the evening and leaves at four in the morning. At home I notice that he keeps the blinds drawn tight, as though he has developed a sensitivity to sunlight. He completed his training on the day shift, where he was informed that one could tell the two categories of employee apart based on looks alone. The day-shifters were tan and athletic, buoyant and cheerful, while the night-shifters were pale and hunched and scurrying. They looked like they survived off role-play video games and soup cups and Joe Rogan. When my brother-in-law's training period ended and he was assigned to the night shift, he tried to not take it personally.

. . .

The factory prints labels. Before my brother-in-law started this job, I did not understand how many types of labels existed. Roll labels, shrink sleeve, thermal transfer, QR code, holographic, pressure sensitive, cold foil stamping. Once I became alert to the world of labels I started noticing them everywhere, wrapped around the sweaty necks of sports drinks and the tin bodies of soup cans, assuring people that they are finding what they seek. A very important business, the making of labels, and so mistakes must be kept to a minimum.

My brother-in-law's predecessor was fired because, instead of catching mistakes, he kept trying to smuggle "666" into the bar codes. The mark of the beast. Word around the factory is that this person was driven mad by the hours he kept on the night shift. Word around the factory is that this person has since abandoned society and joined up with one of the militias we keep hearing about on the news.

On the night shift, people barely talk to each other, even in the break room. Everyone is lodged in their own private dreams. My brother-in-law gets two fifteen-minute reprieves and spends them both outside, stretching his legs in the vast parking lot. By the time that second break arrives, the night sky looks like deep space and the parking lot is so quiet he feels like the last person left on earth. Two night-shifters have recently gone missing. In the parking lot, my brother-in-law wonders if they were outside when they disappeared. If they were standing in the same place, looking up at the same midnight sky. In the factory, flyers bearing the faces and names of the missing night-shifters are taped to corridors and bathroom stalls, thumbtacked to corkboards. This contagion of missingness felt distant at first, but now it is creeping closer. My brother-in-law sees the faces of these two employees so often he sometimes feels as though they have not gone missing at all, but have just wandered away into a distant wing of the factory.

One afternoon, I get a text from my brother-in-law, asking me to come over. "We need to talk," he tells me when I arrive. In the living room, I step around the bright fragments of puzzles scattered across the rug and sit on the couch. Overhead a white ceiling fan spins in listless circles. "Your sister has been acting really strange lately," he says, pacing in front of the couch. "Is she pregnant again?" I ask, and he looks alarmed. He's already in his night shift uniform, a black polo shirt and khaki pants. "It's not that," he says. "Believe me." My brother-in-law has dark curly hair and wide shoulders. When not dressed for work, he favors high-top sneakers and T-shirts from heavy metal bands. In the living room, he tells me that my sister has been spending hours strapped into MIND'S EYE. "I thought meditating was supposed to be a silent activity," my brother-in-law says, "but I can hear her talking. She always shuts the door, but I can still hear her through the walls." When she's out of the house she sometimes doesn't answer her phone for hours, ironic since our sister used to complain, when we were kids, about how hard it could be to reach our mother when she was at work, no matter how much we needed her. At times, the silence stretches on for so long that my brother-in-law is terrified that his wife will become a missing person. He sits down next to me. He pulls out his phone and shows me a covert photo he took of my sister using the device. She's sitting on the floor of their bedroom, legs bent, back straight against the wall. Her mouth is open. Her hands hang limp between her legs. "I think she wants something," he continues. "I think she's searching. I wish I knew what she wanted, or what she's looking for." It seems to me that my sister is undertaking a pilgrimage of some kind, even if the terms are not yet legible to us. "Has she told you about what happens when she uses MIND'S EYE?" I ask my brother-in-law. "Has she told you about our father appearing in the English garden and telling her *There is something I want you to do*?" My brother-in-law slides his phone back into his pocket. He rubs his eyes, which look the same as they always have. He is a rational person. Someone who wants to believe that everything is as it appears to be. "But how can your father want anything?"

my brother-in-law asks me, with the utmost sincerity. "He's dead."

That night, in the attic bedroom, I get an email from the author's assistants. The plot about the retired undercover cop who gets sucked back into the Miami underworld has been altered to include time travel. The villain, an assassin turned drug lord turned mayoral candidate, was taken out by the cop's father in the eighties but has been resurrected and has traveled forward in time to avenge his own killing. By now the cop's father is dead, so the son is the next best target. *Traveled forward in time HOW?* I ask the assistants, but they insist that the details aren't important. The famous author just wants the book to have a little of that eighties *Scarface*-era flair plus a dash of sci-fi. *People love to read about things that are impossible*, the assistants tell me. *And time travel is trending because people are desperate to believe there are other dimensions beyond the one we currently occupy.* I often wonder who these assistants are, how many there are, and why their identities must be kept anonymous. I wonder why their emails always sound the same, as though they are written not by individuals but by a collective. I wonder if they think the same assistant thoughts, eat the same assistant lunches, dream the same assistant dreams.

. . .

As the summer thickens around us we start to notice little changes inside my mother's house. We'll all come back from the grocery and find the front door cracked open or a water glass sitting on the kitchen counter, one that we did not leave there. After my mother goes to bed, my husband and I will walk the dog and, upon our return, notice that someone has hacked away at the mint plant growing wild by the front door or find a head-shaped indentation in our pillows. I wonder if we have managed to acquire a ghost instead of a stoop cat, but then I remember that my sister has a key. One morning, I'm in my mother's yard and hear my sister pulling weeds on the other side of the fence. "Kind of a weird question," I say before asking if she has been coming over surreptitiously, to take a nap or drink a glass of water. I listen to my sister chop away at the earth. "You sound like a fucking psycho right now," she says. Each word is soaked in a fury so hot that I retreat. That night, after my mother goes to sleep, my husband and I take the dog out and we hear singing coming from a derelict house. The house is made of sallow yellow brick, the walls distended as though they are barely holding back something terrible. We stand in front of the house, let the voices pass over us like waves. We peer through the dust-fogged windows and see if we can make out figures moving around inside. Then I look down and notice a small red radio, left out here for whatever reason, the dial turned to a gospel station. Back at my mother's house, we find my sister inside, asleep in a window seat. She is curled up in her work clothes, slacks and a short-sleeved blouse. One kitten heel on her foot and the other at rest on the floor. Her expression so soft and tender, so free of anger, that she could be mistaken for a child playing dress-up. "Who's the psycho now," I say as I wake her. She sits up slowly and yawns wide. I can see the fat white molars in the back of her mouth. "You would not believe the things I've been seeing," she tells me, her voice still thick with sleep. "You mean with MIND'S EYE?" She nods. "It's like a dream," she says, "but also not." I take her hand and tell her that I will absolutely believe the things she's been seeing. Just the other night I dreamed I was in a spaceship with Tony Montana and together we were traveling into the future. I don't tell her that I woke up feeling like something in my body had changed, so I went to the bathroom to check on my belly button and found that I could now stick half a finger inside.

My sister does not want to go home. She wants to go for a drive. When she collects her large leather satchel from the floor I glimpse the smooth white edge of the headset inside. "I don't remember how I got into the house," my sister tells me as we drive. "I don't even remember walking over." She looks out the window and chews on her fingernail. She does not seem angry for once. Just confused and sad. I circle the smooth onyx perimeter of the lake. I feel like we are riding together in a little spaceship, tracing the borders of an alien planet. My sister tells me that she keeps trying to do her favorite MIND'S EYE meditation, the one in the English garden, but our father always interrupts. *There is something I want you to do.* "Maybe you should spend more time in the real world," I tell her, but she shakes her head. The gold flecks in her eyes shimmer. Her nostrils tremble. "I know he is trying to tell me something," she says. "I know there must be a reason he's trying to reach me."

At the Institute, the same orderly worked night shifts. Except on Sundays. Then it was someone else. This all happened many years in the past, but still I think about that orderly whenever my brother-in-law talks about his own night shift at the factory. The orderly was young—mid-twenties—though by virtue of having regular contact with the outside world he seemed full of life experience, knowledge. After a month at the Institute, I stopped sleeping, because the things that happened in the middle of the night were terrifying. My first roommate clawed trenches into her forearms. I woke one morning to find blood spatter all over the blue vinyl floor. Like I had been deposited into a crime scene. She was held down by two orderlies while another cut her nails. The whole time she screamed like an animal on the edge of slaughter. Eventually she was taken away and I never saw her again. My second roommate managed to construct a noose out of bras and underwear. I woke one night and saw her long pale feet suspended above the floor, pointing and flexing like a dancer. At first, I thought I was having a dream that my roommate was floating or that she was possessed. I was so heavily medicated that much of my living was done through my dreams. Then I looked up and saw that her whole body was twitching and her face was purple. It was like waking up in the throes of an earthquake and before you can even stand you are tipped over into some bottomless pit.

There are still foods I cannot eat, because they are so closely associated with that period of my life. Applesauce, apple juice, green peas, Ritz crackers.

That second roommate survived, but damaged her trachea and had to be moved to a different facility. I did not get a third roommate, as though the Institute feared that the problem might be me. At night, I decided I would rather stay awake and vigilant, to be among the first to feel the violent shaking of the earth.

After two weeks, my parents were permitted to visit me. It was a horror, I soon realized, to have people from the outside world appear in the world of the Institute. All it did was remind me of the reality I had left behind, the reality that they would, after the visit ended, rejoin with ease. The reality I might not ever see again. I can remember the flush and pinch of my mother's face and her sturdy, concerned voice. The same tone I'd heard her take with social work clients on the phone. My father brought me a Snickers bar and a copy of *Seventeen*, even though both were forbidden. "Please don't come back," I begged them the next time I was permitted to call home. My mother was all too happy to honor my request, but my father still showed up from time to time, usually outside the narrow window allotted to visitors— somehow he was able to sweet-talk the staff—and carrying some form of benign contraband. Before leaving, he'd slap me on the shoulder and quote John Wayne. *Courage is being scared to death but saddling up anyway.* My only other visitor was my high school English teacher. I was surprised: I had never been an attentive student, though I had expressed to her a vague interest in writing. Nevertheless, one afternoon she made the drive to see me. She arrived in a long skirt, a short-sleeved blouse, sensible clogs. She reeked so power- fully of the outside world that I started to sob. In the com- munity room, she put her hand on my arm and began listing all the famous writers who spent time in institutions. Ten- nessee Williams, Robert Lowell, Sylvia Plath, Anne Sexton. "Sometimes," she said, "there is a price to pay for being a ge- nius." I asked my English teacher if I was, in her estimation, a genius and she told me it was too soon to say for sure. "You can't follow instructions to save your life. You daydream. You seem full of disorder. These are all promising signs."

When the night shift orderly cracked open my door for room checks, he always found me awake, sitting on my bed and staring at the ceiling or reading the *Oxford English Diction- ary*, the only thing I had found of interest in the Institute's modest library. The other titles were self-help books of the most odious nature. On the night shift, the orderly always asked me for a word of the day and I was happy to oblige. I would spend hours searching for a good word. *Ovulite, n. A fossil of ovoidal form and uncertain identity. Astrogator, n. A person who navigates a vehicle through space. Freshet, n. A flood or overflowing of a river caused by heavy rains or melted snow.* On occasion, the night shift orderly questioned the *OED*'s entries. I would turn the entry around, so the page faced him. He would lean into the room and squint, but always kept a respectful distance from my bed, as though he knew there was an invisible barrier that he could not cross.

In the beginning, I took this as a sign that he meant no harm.

In the attic room, I submit my chapters for the Miami-underworld-time-travel novel; within hours I get a reply from the assistants, even though we're in the dead of night. I assume they're writing to point out my mistakes. Too many concrete descriptive details and not enough adverbs! Too many em dashes and too few ellipses! *Everything is not as it seems—* vs. *Everything is not as it seems . . .* The assistants believe that em dashes are abrupt, mysterious, foreboding. Ellipses, meanwhile, are an enticing trail of bread crumbs. A hand reaching out from the shadowed night. The job of the assistants is not so different from my brother-in-law's job at the factory; they are both in the business of catching mistakes. As it happens, the assistants are already sending over my next assignment. A much faster turnaround than usual. When I open the document, I find a blank page. *You attached the wrong file,* I write, pleased to be able to point out their error for once. How satisfying it must be for my brother-in-law to catch all those mistakes in a great net and hurl them back into the midnight sea of the factory. The sky has paled to lavender. Soon dawn will creep in behind the trees. The branches will glow as if lit from within and my brother-in-law will begin his journey home. My sister and my niece are asleep next door. My husband and our dog and my mother are all asleep below me, bundled up in their own private dreamworlds. I don't think my father gets to dream anymore, though I would be happy to be wrong about that. Maybe everything is a dream for him now, full of puzzling transitions and gentle doom.

My email pings. It is 5:45 a.m. When do these assistants sleep?

Not a mistake, the assistants reply. *Quite the opposite. He wants to see what you can do.*

The Wilderness

By late June my husband has run seven hundred miles. Roughly the distance a citizen in medieval Europe might traverse for a pilgrimage. Nine hundred miles from Lyon to Compostela. Six hundred from Toulouse to Canterbury. He has amassed a cheering section on his route. From a preacher—he lives in a camper van with DERMA, MISSISSIPPI painted on the side in red letters—there are regular offers of beer and God. From the woman who passes out religious pamphlets, regular offers of water and God. "Keep it tight," the bike man always says. Two white women with languorous accents cruise the road that runs parallel to the lake in an old baby-blue Peugeot, all four windows rolled down, a missing-person sign secured to the rear windshield. "You look real good, baby," the women call out. "Keep it up, baby." When the local sheriff passes in her squad car, she addresses my husband over her speaker. "There's my running man!" At first, the attention made him feel self-conscious, but by now he has given himself over to being cheered. He thinks of his fans when the summer air is a hot brick in his lungs and he wants to quit; he thinks about how he does not want to let these people down. Now that he's out of a job, I suggest he consider running for mayor. He's gotten to know the whole town and everyone seems to think he's a hero, just for running. He could wear his campaign shirt down by the lake, we joke. I even come up with a slogan: RUNNING FOR THE PEOPLE.

I know for a fact that my husband has become famous down here, because perfect strangers approach me to remark on his running. They tell me that he waves to them, that he calls out good morning, that he motivates them to continue with their own exercise. How the sweat flies from his body! And still he keeps running! An older couple in matching white visors stop me in the Publix and tell me that they've started walking a mile on the lake each morning, just to see my husband. Most people don't know his name, so they just call him "the running man." No one knows my name either, unless they're friends with my sister or my mother. They just know that I'm married to "the running man." I can only assume that they have seen us out together, walking the dog. We must be an easy pair to remember because I'm white and he's Korean American and we haven't seen too many East Asian people around here. Your husband runs so far! people tell me. He is always smiling, people tell me. It's good that he's keeping up his strength, people tell me. It's amazing, people tell me. He doesn't even carry water.

One morning, my husband reports that the truck man has resurfaced down by the lake and is now accompanied by a sorrel hound. Lean with a silvered snout. On his run, he saw dog and human sitting together on the truck bed (the rear tire has recovered from the stabbing). They were by the park, where the clusters of missing-person signs have continued to grow, commandeering the grass like an invasive species. On this particular morning the faces of the vanished looked as open and tender as flowers. The truck man was drinking a beer and stroking the hound's head when the bike man walked past with his white dog. The hound jumped down from the truck bed. The white dog strained against his lead; the animals touched noses. The two men didn't say anything to each other. The bike man just nodded and walked on. My husband wonders if this might be the beginning of a truce.

On the last day in June, I get a call from my sister. "You'll never guess where I am," she says, and before I can attempt any guesses she tells me, "The woods." I reply that there are woods all over and she is going to have to get more specific. She explains that she just finished inspecting a property— a roof damaged by a fallen tree—in a neighborhood where a childhood friend used to live. "We searched for you for hours," my sister tells me. "We thought you had been abducted, like those kids on the backs of milk cartons. Finally we found you in the woods." By now I know the memory she's revisiting. Once, we went to this childhood friend's house for a sleepover and I staged my first attempt at running away. I was ten and a powerful voice inside me called out *go, go, go.* "It was the neighborhood that got me thinking," my sister continues. "I haven't been out here in a long time." She tells me that she stomped through the grass in her heels, past a playground with a swing set, the metal chains creaking. The trees still looked like ordinary trees, a scrubby wall of green. At ten, I had a little pink backpack with white tassels, and before running away I loaded it up with Goldfish crackers taken from my friend's kitchen. I wandered the neighborhood for a while before I found the playground and the woods. I went from tree to tree, slapping each truck with an open hand, until my legs got tired and I sat down. I ate some Goldfish crackers and wished I had remembered water. I fell asleep and when I woke back up I could hear people nearby, calling my name. "Why were you so unhappy?" my sister asks me, her voice tight. "Why did you want to get away from me so badly?" My sister also wants to believe that there is a clear answer for every question, that things are always what they appear to be. I think this must be because our parents kept so many secrets; we could feel them lurking below the surface of our lives, like reef sharks gliding beneath snorkelers. A silent and terrifying mass. "Ten is a mysterious age," I tell her. "It wasn't for me," my sister says. "Back then everything was perfectly clear." I hear the acid creep into her voice and attempt to change the subject. I ask her what the sky is like right now and she pauses. A rustling sound, as though she is standing in a light wind or handling a paper bag. "The clouds are large and strangely shaped." Then she hangs up. I try to call her back. Instead of answering she texts me two photos:

a massive white cloud passing like a zeppelin overhead and a sandy shade-dark footpath that leads into the woods. In reality this area is a homely three acres of slash pine and cabbage palm. Back then it only seemed big because I was so small. Still, each time my sister said "woods" I heard "wilderness." I imagine my sister standing on the border of a great wilderness. The wilderness our father disappeared into. That I nearly disappeared into. The wilderness we can burn but never bury.

Pour my sister a glass of wine when she gets home, I start to text my brother-in-law, but then I remember that he is already at the factory. *Pour yourself a glass of wine when you get home*, I text my sister. Seconds later, she replies with a heart emoji.

In the bathroom, I raise my T-shirt and examine my belly button. In the mirror, the indentation looks like a regular belly button, but when I press on it the skin parts and my fingers vanish into a shallow tunnel. I wonder if my body is growing a second vagina and if that would be a gift or a nightmare. I withdraw my fingers and sniff the curve of a nail. I get the faint scent of wax, fresh-cut grass, the sea.

Later that night, in the attic bedroom, I listen to a storm threaten outside. Thunder, wind. I sit at my laptop. Ever since my new assignment came through, I have been staring down the same blank page. I am unaccustomed to this amount of freedom. I am a novice swimmer attempting to paddle herself across the ocean—which is to say I've been given just enough freedom to drown in. Making up a plot, even a ridiculous one, sounds easy until you actually have to do it. I must admit that I feel a new and grudging respect for the famous author. Eventually I climb down from the attic, defeated, and join my husband in bed. Then, in the middle of the night, an idea arrives in a dream. Tony Montana and I are back in the spaceship. We have, for some inexplicable reason, traveled backward in time to the Ice Age and we have barely escaped with our lives. Tony Montana's shirt is half-unbuttoned and soaked in blood; his black hair is fringed with ice. *Stop acting like a little bitch*, Tony Montana tells me, *and write the story of what happened when you were at the Institute.* Those are his last words before he slumps over dead. *Of course!* I think when I wake up. I don't have to invent a plot after all. I only have to get out of bed and begin.

In my last month at the Institute, I was troubled by the same dream. I was floating underwater. The water was translucent and very blue, like a gemstone that was bright but also lucent. Aquamarine, tourmaline, opalite. The body of water was vast—an ocean or perhaps an enormous lake; the particulars were not available to me—and I was staring up through the undulating surface and into the actual sky, where oblong white clouds moved swiftly, like tectonic plates in the process of rearranging themselves.

I should have been afraid of drowning, but I was not. Also, I felt no need to blink.

What terrified me about the dream was that when I went to move I found that I could not. I was being held in place by some invisible force, and I was excruciatingly aware of everything that was happening to me.

On occasion, I would hear the distant whir of a motor and think *help is here*, but no one would ever come.

To be clear, I had not acquired the ability to breathe underwater. It was as though my lungs had been temporarily stilled—the lobes, the alveoli, the bronchioles that branch out like fingers of coral—and I was being kept alive by some other mechanism.

I lose steam after a few pages. I don't know where to go after describing the dream itself. I google "how to start a novel" and learn that one should never begin a novel with a dream.

. . .

First thing in the morning my brother-in-law calls. By then I've abandoned the davenport for a cushion on the floor, hoping the change in location might resurrect the momentum that visited me in the middle of the night, but all I have is a legal pad littered with em dashes. "Hey," he says, "is your sister with you?" I look around the attic room like my sister might have snuck in here without me noticing. I go downstairs and walk through my mother's house, hoping I will find her on the sofa or in the love seat, sleeping the morning away like a character in a fairy tale. My husband has already left for his run. The dog follows me from one room to the next, nails clicking on the floor. I go outside and stand on the sidewalk, where I am held by a dread so powerful I don't even notice the flaming hot concrete on my bare feet. I look around at the other houses. I look at a paper bag being carried down the street by the wind. I look up at the sky: something has gone strange in the atmosphere. The sky is very low and veined with charcoal; the dark lines undulate like tentacles. On the other end of the call, I hear the rumble of the TV and my niece screaming like a creature in a birds of prey exhibit. "Well?" my brother-in-law says. "Is she?"

EVERYTHING IS
NOT AS IT SEEMS

JULY 1–14

Floods

The day my sister is reported missing, rain starts falling in thick blue sheets. Five inches in the first hour. On TV, the meteorologists are bewildered. The Doppler shows no sign of a hurricane, the violent masses of red and orange that tangle and swell and churn, monsters lurching toward the next site of destruction. There is only a sepia haze over the entire state, like a veil no one can figure out how to lift. The meteorologists have no idea what to call the storm, so they settle on A Major Weather Event. The three of us—my mother and husband and I—huddle in front of the TV. The dog whines at our feet. We feel the light bathe our faces. We act as though the TV is an oracle and we are awaiting divine instruction. Twenty inches now and the water gushes over the edges of lakes and rivers; the ocean crashes past seawalls, floods streets. In the Panhandle, my half brother has checked into the top floor of a hotel, abandoning his guiding outfit to the encroaching militias. No part of the state will be spared. "If you have a canoe or a kayak or a raft, if you have really any kind of vessel at all, then this would be the time to use it," advises a meteorologist on the news.

That night, we stand in front of the living room windows and watch the falling rain. My mother has a backup generator, so the house is still illuminated, but the lights are a pale, flickering yellow and the machine makes a dreadful roar; it sounds like an act of annihilation is occurring in the back-yard. We are all familiar with hurricanes, with the summer thunderstorms that rage for hours, but this is different. There is no thunder or lightning or wind. There is only water bear-ing down so forcefully it sounds like we're standing under massive falls. "Yes, it really is still raining," my husband says, when my father-in-law calls to see if the weather is as dire as the news anchors in New Jersey are claiming. "No, we really don't know where she is."

Florida has more waterways—more rivers, more channels—than any other state in America. Over a thousand miles of coastline. In 1928, the Okeechobee Hurricane claimed twenty-five hundred lives after dikes were overcome by the storm surge. In 1992, Hurricane Andrew drowned seventy thousand acres of trees in the Everglades, killed sixty-five people, caused $25 billion in damage. In 2017, Hurricane Irma left nearly 75 percent of the state without power, hud-dled in the heat and in the dark. Florida is used to disaster, in other words, but it is used to disasters it can name.

My sister is an expert in disaster, thanks to her work as a claims adjuster. In the attic room, I find myself sifting through her many stories, like the one about the homeowner who tried to convince her that his parrot was the one who carried a lit cigarette upstairs and left it smoldering on the floor, right by the highly flammable drapes. Or the woman who flooded her own basement with a garden hose. I think of my sister's electrum eyes and the smooth white curve of the MIND'S EYE headset in her satchel and our strange late-night drive around the lake. What part of the story are we in right now? Are we in the middle, or are we still at the beginning? Is the end closer than we think? I find these to be surprisingly difficult questions to answer.

Chaucer is believed to be the first Western writer to use the phrase "mind's eye" in a work of literature. This is one of the many useless facts that I remember from my abandoned dissertation. The dictionary definition of "mind's eye" goes: *the mental faculty of conceiving imaginary or recollected scenes.* The mind's eye is all about memory, in other words. It is about how we construct our lives inside ourselves. That most private of architectures.

When we were children, my sister and I had a babysitter who collected us from school and half-heartedly supervised us until our parents returned from work. This babysitter loved to read the tabloids. When she was finished, I would fish them out of the trash, lock myself in a bathroom, and study them with the awe typically reserved for a holy text. I read all about Hillary Clinton's alien baby. About Tonya Harding and Lorena Bobbitt. Those tabloids loved stories about dangerous women. In the summer of 1994, Nicole Brown Simpson's and Ron Goldman's blood-drenched bodies were on every cover. That was the first time I ever saw a dead body, as I sat alone on the toilet seat, turning the pages of the *National Enquirer*. Several years ago, my sister got a call from this babysitter, now in her fifties. She asked my sister to meet for coffee. My sister remembered this babysitter fondly and agreed. At a café, the babysitter told my sister that I abused her when we were children. "Don't you remember?" she said. "She made you lick her shoes. She put a dog collar and a leash on you and hauled you around like an animal." When my sister relayed this conversation, I was shocked. I had, sincerely, no memory of committing these offenses. Stranger still, my sister—who has never been reticent about airing her grievances—had no memory of these things being done to her. In the end, it was our word against the babysitter's. Maybe our own memories shielded us from these events. Maybe the babysitter had become deranged, after all those decades of tabloid consumption. Was she attempting to turn us against each other? Or had she somehow confused us with another family? Of course, the most alarming possibility was that the babysitter was right— because, if that was the case, what else were we not remembering? It always amazes me when people ask *what happened?* as though the question is a simple one.

· · ·

No one can go outside, because of the Major Weather Event. We cannot search the wilderness or anywhere else that my sister might have gone. We have filed a missing-person report with the police, but they have been inundated with missing people all summer and now the first floor of the local station has flooded. We have tried calling and texting my sister a million times over, but that doesn't stop me from staying up all night and flinging missives into the abyss. I imagine this is how my sister must have felt when I bolted to Tallahassee, a constant, sloshing gut-sickness. In the upstairs bathroom, I strip down in front of the mirror and examine my belly button. The hole has gotten deep enough that I can tuck a small item inside. Earlier I slipped a dime into the little pouch and carried it around all day, just for some extra company. Now I pull the dime out and hold it up to the light. The coin is warm and sticky, but otherwise unharmed. I place the coin on the edge of the sink and take a tube of ChapStick from a drawer. I pry open my belly button and slide the ChapStick inside. I feel a tightness around my stomach, a swift ripple of pain, and then the muscles relax. How useful it could be to store a few little things inside my very own body. Like ChapStick or my house key. Things that I am always losing, always struggling to find.

My father-in-law calls to say he is watching the rich get airlifted from the peaks of luxury high-rises in Miami. In New Jersey, the news anchors are speculating that Florida has brought this flood upon itself, spiritually speaking, considering everything that has gone wrong down here. My husband takes the call in our bedroom, staring out at the falling rain. After he hangs up, I stand beside him. Our dog wedges his soft body between us, furrows his golden brow, and growls at the churning weather. "We need to talk about your mother," my husband says. He tells me that every time he goes downstairs my mother corners him in the kitchen and starts going on about utopias. "She told me about the etymology of 'utopia,'" he says. "How the word literally translates to 'no place.' How the hardest thing about building a utopia is imagining something that does not yet exist. I think, because I study pilgrimages, she is under the impression that I'll understand what she's talking about." He starts to jog in place, arms pumping and knees lifting high. Apparently my mother spoke in detail about a utopian novel called *The Great Romance*, published anonymously in 1881. The protagonist falls asleep and wakes up hundreds of years later and discovers that everyone in society has developed telepathic abilities. The cultivation of telepathy has greatly improved the moral order, as people can no longer conceal toxic secrets and evil plans. I'm a little horrified by this vision of a utopian society, as is usually the case. How are all these telepathic people supposed to develop an inner life? There is a suspicious lack of privacy in many of these utopias.

· · ·

Here is a fact about my mother that very few people know: she spent time in an institution too, a hospital, for six months when she was eighteen. She was part of an experimental drug trial. Her room, like mine, did not have a window, and so, unless a nurse came by and told her the weather, she had no idea about the state of the outdoors. She passed the time by reading huge quantities of books and smoking the cigarettes sold by candy stripers. I suspect the time my mother spent in that hospital has something to do with her current fascination with utopias. The rigid rules, the isolation, the lack of privacy. It must all seem very familiar to her. Sometimes we are called back to the things we most want to flee, perhaps because they left such a mark that we don't know how to leave them behind. Sometimes I feel this way about the Institute, that the longer I stay in Florida the more a reencounter of some kind seems inevitable—and maybe this is a desire I've been nurturing, in secret, all along. Perhaps we think we can destroy the places of our past by returning: by reimagining, rebuilding. A utopia is, after all, a thing that rises from disaster, ruin, rubble. Without all that failure there can be no such thing as a utopia, since there would be no other reality to compare it to.

When I was at the Institute all I wanted was to escape, but once I was discharged staying away was much harder than I had anticipated. First, there was the matter of the night shift orderly and the way our relationship spilled outside the bounds of the Institute, the hold he continued to have on me. Eventually he went to work elsewhere and we lost touch, but that did not stop me from going back one night with my best friend at the time, the girl I met in the outpatient therapy group. The girl who loved to talk about knives and what she planned to use them for. The girl who would become a woman and be lost to the wilderness. One afternoon, the two of us drove down to Pompano Beach. The Institute is in Fort Lauderdale; all day I could feel the place breathing down my neck. My friend had straight, dark hair that fell to her waist, an oiled tan, ice-blue eyes. That day she wore a tiny white string bikini. "Definitely not drowning," she said at one point, gazing out at the ocean. "Too big a chance of some do-gooder getting involved." After she died, one thing I would remember is how much she loved *Baywatch*. She had seen each episode multiple times and could recite the opening credits from memory. *Our team is the elite of the elite.* By the time we left Pompano Beach it was dark. I asked my friend if she wanted to take a detour. We drove over to the Institute. We parked on the edge of the lot. By then I knew the night shift orderly no longer worked there, but still I imagined him roaming the hallway with his flashlight, making his rounds. "So this is the place?" she asked me as we got out. "Yeah," I said. "This is the place." I told her that an orderly fell in love with me while I was there. I told her that he stalked me for a while, after I got out. "So fucked up," my friend whispered in the dark. "People tell us we're sick and then they use that as an excuse to do whatever they want." I wanted to commit an act of vandalism. I wanted to hurt this place the way it had hurt me, but I knew if I smashed a window all kinds of alarms would sound. In the end, we found a hose coiled in the back of the building. We turned it on and left the water to gush, wasteful and childish, but at the time I allowed myself to imagine the water rushing in under the doors, filling the rooms and levitating the furniture, a flood.

The hospital is a period from my mother's life that she has never been willing to discuss, despite our shared histories of confinement. All I know is that she had an illness and the drug trial presented her with the possibility of a cure. But what kind of illness? What kind of cure? Once, after my parents divorced, I put these questions to my father. "She told you she was in there for a drug trial?" he said. We were having lunch at a deli. He held half a sandwich in midair and smirked. "Your mother likes to believe she's very special." When I asked my father why my mother was there, if not for a drug trial, he said I should ask her, and when I did ask her, she said my father was a son of a bitch and locked herself in her bedroom. More sinkholes in our family story. The only memory from that time she ever shares is of how she was in the hospital when Kennedy was shot. She knew something awful had happened when she heard the nurses screaming their lungs out in the hallway, though quite a bit of time passed before someone came to tell her what.

. . .

Once, at the Institute, I asked a counselor why the library didn't have any novels and he said that invented worlds over-stimulated the imagination. The counselors regarded the imaginations of their patients as a herd of stampeding animals: in need of sedation, calming down. In my last month there, I found a novel called *Time and Again* stuffed behind a toilet like contraband. I did not take the book from its hiding place; instead, I kept it stashed behind the toilet and would read a chapter whenever I used that particular stall. The novel is about an illustrator in New York City who is recruited to participate in "the project," which uses self-hypnosis to send people backward through time. I don't remember very much about the mechanics of the time travel, but I do remember the illustrator talking about how his life had a big gaping hole in it and that he was at a loss for how to fill it, or even for understanding what belonged in there.

In Florida, there are two towns called Utopia. One is located in Sarasota County and the other is to the south, in Broward County. Every hurricane season, for the last five years, both of these Utopias have been ravaged by storms.

When I first became a ghost, the assistants emailed me a tip sheet titled *Principles of Plot*. From this sheet, I learned that every action in a story is caused by what precedes it. Nothing is random, in other words. We are all existing in the cradle of a great narrative design. Every action has a consequence; every consequence has a response. In the plots the famous author devises, the actions and the consequences are usually the product of individual grudges and failings and desires, but these days I can't help but feel as though Florida is in the grip of something far more colossal. That the actions and the consequences and the responses are all too numerous, too long running, to even list. That the narrative cradle is cracking apart. That we are all responding, we are overflowing with response, even if we have lost track of what exactly we are responding to.

On the third day of the flood, my brother-in-law and niece move into my mother's house. He did not want to leave his house, in case my sister returned, but he does not have a backup generator and the rooms have turned into steaming caves. He says that, at night, without power or streetlights, the darkness got so thick, so viscous and physical, he thought it might eat them alive. "I will never look at that house in the same way," he says. "Now that I know what really lives in there." Also, my mother is situated at the top of the street, on a slight rise, the threshold set back from the curb. At the moment, the shimmering gray water is only lapping at the yard. My husband and I find a two-seater kayak in my mother's garage and tether it to the front porch, as the

flooded streets have rendered our cars useless. "Noah?" my
niece asks whenever she peers outside, because our governor,
the Cro-Magnon in a suit, recently passed a bill dismantling
the teaching of American history in public schools. Teach-
ers are now encouraged to replace those lessons with biblical
stories. "Let's hope not," I reply. I don't think this town could
survive forty days and forty nights. As it is, we have to turn
the generator off periodically, to conserve fuel. My mother
has scheduled a "no generator" zone from noon to five; during these hours, the heat pools on the floors, creeps up the
walls. It surrounds us. It buries us alive. We lie around for
hours and drip sweat. My niece tells me that she is worried
about her pet ghost. The ghost eats dirt, but now all the dirt
looks like soup. "Can ghosts drown?" she wants to know. I
tuck my hands under her hot armpits and hoist her into the
air, something I have seen my sister do when she wants to
distract my niece from whatever danger is unfolding in the
outside world. "Are you a bird?" I ask her. "Or a plane?" My
niece stares down at me with her dark round eyes. She balls
her tiny fists and starts to wail.

That afternoon, my husband and I kayak around the neighborhood and search for my sister. I sit up front. He sits in the
back, acts as our anchor. It is dizzying to see familiar sights—
the windows of a neighbor's house, a telephone pole, a white
steeple—from an alien vantage. I don't want to imagine my
sister trapped underneath all this water, so I look high, at

roofs and treetops. I imagine her clinging to a church steeple or perched in the canopy of an oak tree, her green-gold
eyes flashing like two tiny searchlights. Instead I find half
a dozen cats, mewling, claws dug into the heavy branches.
We try to coax the cats down into the kayak, but they bare
their teeth and hiss. The field of missing persons must also
be submerged, since we keep spotting faces floating in the
oily water. With the paddle I touch the image of a man with
a ginger mustache, missing thirty-eight days; I watch his expression dissolve. We find a golf ball, a kitchen sponge, a
prosthetic hand. A paperback drifts by and I recognize the
title. *Season of Death.* It's one of the famous author's early
novels, published many years before I joined his ghostwriting enterprise. Back when the famous author used to actually write his own books. I lean over and fish *Season of Death*
out of the water. A small motorized boat passes, piloted by
a couple in goggles, white T-shirts tied around their heads.
The kayak sways in the wake.

One of my husband's favorite pilgrim stories is that of Saint
Brendan of Clonfert, an Irish seafaring pilgrim who later became a saint. For his pilgrimage, Saint Brendan of Clonfert
gathered fourteen monks and set out for the Promised Land
for Saints. At the last minute, three additional passengers
joined; Saint Brendan of Clonfert prophesied that these interlopers would never return to Ireland, because seventeen
is an unholy number. Brendan and his followers spent seven

years at sea. Periodically, they came upon an island, such as the Island of Sheep and the Island of Birds and the Island of Strong Men, where one of the interlopers was carried away by demons. It was as though each island was a gateway to a different world. After seven years of searching, they finally reached the Promised Land for Saints, where they were welcomed and allowed a brief stay.

In Ireland, the site where Saint Brendan of Clonfert was baptized is visited often by pilgrims seeking physical and mental consolation.

I think of Saint Brendan as we paddle past houses ringed with water. Island of tchotchkes. Island of baby strollers. Island of overdue library books. Island of hunting trophies. Island of orchids. Island of fentanyl. Island of seashell collections in cut-glass bowls. Island of pet snakes. Island of formal photo portraits of distant ancestors.

In the end, my husband and I find no trace of my sister, but we do rescue a neighbor from her roof. We find her straddling the ridge and waving a pink scarf. At home, my mother gets out a sleeping bag, a spare pillow, canned soup. We learn the rescued neighbor isn't even technically a neighbor. She did a swap with a cousin, who is presently at her house in

Arizona. The house swap is supposed to end in two days but now there is no telling when she will be able to leave. Arizona wears a knit tie-dyed crop top and black basketball shorts. She has a blond pixie cut and a nose ring. "Fucking Florida," Arizona says as she unrolls her sleeping bag on the living room floor.

In the attic bedroom, I open *Season of Death* and lay it face down on the desk to dry. When I was first hired, the assistants told me to not bother with the early books in the famous author's oeuvre, as those books represented a style he has since abandoned. "Nascent efforts," they called the early works. The cover of *Season of Death* is black and shiny. The title and the author's name are embossed in a large red font. At the bottom, a figure races into the distance. I can't tell anything about this person, what they might be running away from or toward. A net of ambiguity cast so wide it becomes meaningless.

Later that night, an email from the assistants arrives. They want a progress update; I want an extension. *For what reason?* I tell them there is an epidemic of missing persons, an epidemic to which my sister now belongs, and also the entire state has flooded. *We're on an ER generator. It's all I can do to keep my cell phone half-charged. And you're in Palm Beach.* On the news, we've seen cars in South Florida drifting down submerged highways like wind-up toys. *Aren't you freaking out?* The assistants are unmoved by the various emergencies plaguing Florida, as though they are navigating an altogether different reality. They demand to see what I have written so far, to prove I don't have writer's block. In the attic room, I read over what I wrote in the hours before my sister vanished and am filled with a lurching disappointment. The assistants are right: I don't have anything to submit. Because what I have written is an account, and not a story. And I want to write a story while I still can.

It is always fascinating, the assistants say in response to my silence, *to see how people choose to make use of their freedom.*

That night, the generator dies. The attic bedroom is plunged into a steaming, airless dark. I switch on a battery-operated lantern and place it on the desk. Sleep is impossible, so I start unpacking my mother's plastic boxes. I find a leather photo album. I hold it in my lap and turn the stiff pages. I stare down at a photo of me as a toddler, fully clothed in a swimming pool. From the angle of the photo, it looks like I'm face down, that the picture was shot underwater, but I know that can't be right. I know I must be floating on my back, with the picture taken from above. At first I think it's an artifact from swimming lessons, but I'm in denim overalls and a long-sleeved shirt, pink socks and white tennis shoes. My eyes are closed. My tiny arms are frozen at peculiar angles. My hair is a flaxen swirl around my head. If I didn't know better—if I weren't right here in the attic bedroom, alive—I might understand this to be a photograph of a drowned child. I'm so disturbed by the swimming pool photo that I put the album away. I notice a white shape in another plastic box and remember the MIND'S EYE headset that was delivered to our house. I unpack the bright white helmet and turn it over in my hands. I slide the straps down over my skull. I don't have to press a single button; the device is activated by human contact. There is a light whirring sound, a quick shock of light. The device is scanning my iris; it is learning me. This MIND'S EYE is fully charged. Five meditations have been preloaded. I think, *English garden.* The world my sister kept disappearing into before she disappeared for real.

A swoop of vertigo, as if I have just stepped off a boat after many hours at sea. I blink. I am standing in front of a white garden gate. The gate is already half-open. An invitation. *Walk,* I think. I start down a gravel path. The tiny pebbles are as smooth and bright as pearls. The path is narrow, winding, bordered by large, ultrabright blooms. Yellow roses, pink peonies, purple hyacinths. I'm awed by how real everything appears. It seems impossible that I am still in the attic, in the throes of a Major Weather Event; I am indeed someplace else. *Go where you need to be.* The MIND'S EYE founder has said that no one will experience the meditations in the exact same way, and I wonder about the differences between my sister's *where* and mine. Here, the sky is a plush baby blue. I can't see the sun, but I can feel it, a pleasant heat on my cheeks and arms. I can smell the sweet fragrance of the flowers. I bend down and pluck a soft petal from the fat pink face of a tea rose. The flower trembles and hisses, like a pot on boil. I step back, the petal crushed in my hand, and watch the tea rose curl into a tight pink fist and then burst open, a fresh blossom springing up from the filament. There is a beauty to this place and also a desolation; I sense I am the only person around for miles. I can no longer feel the sweltering heat of the attic room. I can no longer hear the rain pouring down. There is, instead, a perfect silence. The silence does not feel passive, a mere absence of noise. It feels hungry, alert.

Dad, I think, but nothing happens.

I catch my reflection in a small puddle and it is not an avatar, an animated version of myself—I look as I do in the real world. I touch a finger to the puddle; the water is strangely warm. I watch my reflection wobble.

I pick up a gleaming white pebble. I slide the pebble between my teeth. I roll it around. I feel the smooth texture on my tongue. I taste grass, salt. I bite down. The pebble breaks apart inside my mouth. I swallow the dust.

. . .

I have the curious feeling that I have just eaten a little tooth.

I cannot explain why I put the pebble in my mouth. Something else is in control.

I continue on until I reach a bench. I sit down. The path in front of me dead-ends at a low stone wall covered in ivy; in the distance, I see an apple orchard, the branches heavy with red globes. Beyond the orchard I can make out rolling green fields. A landscape that appears to sprawl out into infinity. *Is this really where I need to be?* The hot and hungry silence is the only response. After a while, I become distracted by the stone wall. There is something wrong with the ivy. The movement of the leaves—a tiny jerking motion, slight yet unsettling—holds my attention. Is this a glitch in the simulation? I stand up from the bench and walk over to the wall. I lean in closer.

In the English garden the air is perfectly still, but the ivy won't stop trembling.

Portals

At the Institute, I lost all sense of time, or at least I lost my understanding of time as it exists in the wider world. There were no more Mondays or Wednesdays or weekends. There was only "craft day" and "group therapy day" and "movie night." After two months at the Institute, I also lost my sense of what constituted normal human behavior. I didn't blink when the person beside me in group talked about being gang-raped by her cousins or when the person across from me at breakfast kept spitting out her food until two staff members hauled her away to be force-fed or when a fellow patient confessed to hiding meds in her vaginal canal or when someone lay down on the ground and simply refused to move. Looking back, I think shock must have driven me into some kind of emotional hibernation; an integral part of my circuitry simply shut down.

Two times a week, we engaged in something called "anger work" where a counselor padded a wall with oversize mauve pillows. The patient was then given a foam baseball bat, neon yellow with a black handle, and was instructed to beat the pillows and scream. The idea being that at least some of our maladies—addiction, depression, dissociation, PTSD, body dysmorphia, hallucinations, suicidal ideation—were products of an unholy rage that had been funneled inward and now that rage would be expelled, as in an exorcism.

"You drink because you hate yourself," the counselor once said to me. "And you hate yourself because someone hurt you."

Because Florida hurt me, I used to think, as though a place could be held responsible.

During "anger work," the patient was blindfolded. The counselor believed the blindfold to be a portal; it would help us teleport back in time, to the moment of the original wound.

You have been tasked with saving our lives, I wanted to say to the counselors, *and this is the best you can come up with? A room filled with hideous mauve pillows, a foam bat, and a blindfold?*

Once the patient was in a state of rage, the counselor would get on her hands and knees and crawl toward the patient and begin to wrestle them. She would put her arms around the patient and try to press them to the ground and the patient would have to fight back. The whole thing was a spectacle and each of these spectacles had an audience, as we all observed the anger work sessions of our fellow patients. We huddled together and watched the anger work subject turn animal. We watched them froth and bleat and howl. I felt that the anger work debased us, and maybe that was the point. The counselors needed to draw out our rawest and vilest selves, for all to see, so they could justify the ways—both subtle and unsubtle—we were dehumanized by life at the Institute.

Cindy was the anger work counselor. She had permed hair and buff arms. She wore green cat-eye glasses. She smelled of spearmint gum. Once, I watched a patient, an anorexic alcoholic who could not have weighed more than eighty pounds, hurl Cindy across the room. Cindy landed against a row of mauve pillows. She straightened her glasses and got back on all fours, undaunted. This was what she wanted to see, after all: the gushing, unmediated rage. If the rage was getting out, the theory went, then it could not get back in. The patient clawed at Cindy's arms. She snatched the glasses off Cindy's face and snapped them in two. I was astonished that someone so small could be so strong. *I told you*, the anorexic alcoholic hissed. *Touch me again and you're fucking dead.* The patients watched Cindy slap at the carpeted floor, in search of her glasses. After that, she started showing up to anger work sessions in long-sleeved shirts and contacts.

. . .

After the rage was expelled, we were supposed to collapse in a lathered exhaustion and weep. At that point, Cindy would wrap her arms around the patient and rock them, as if we were all her children and only she knew how to soothe us.

I think the night shift orderly must have known when anger work was on the schedule, because on those nights he approached me with a fresh gentleness. On one such night, he told me that "quiescent" was a synonym for "calm," though when I looked the word up for myself I learned it actually meant to be immobile, inert, asleep. Later I told him that one must be conscious in order to be calm. That these kinds of distinctions mattered.

The Institute kept me for ten months. The better part of a year. I turned twenty behind its walls. When the time came for me to be discharged, I could not understand the reasoning—I did not, in any way, feel cured—but the staff assured me that a profound change had taken place. A month later, my sister turned seventeen. The year was 2004. That hurricane season, Florida got slammed by four storms in six weeks. Our mother hosted a party, with cake and a piñata made to resemble George W. Bush. When it was my turn to hit the piñata, my mother tied a blindfold tight around my head. I smelled bleach, blood, and foul, unwashed bodies.

Stale air, old carpeting. The sweet musk of apple juice. I was no longer in my mother's backyard. I had been returned to the Institute, to the anger work room, where I could feel Cindy's small, muscled hands crawling all over my body. She was wrestling me to the floor. She was telling me to scream. Someone handed me a baseball bat and I started swinging like I was fending off a serial murderer. The other partygoers had been tentative; perhaps they had mixed feelings about thrashing the likeness of the current president, even if he was a warmongering idiot. When the blindfold was lifted from my face, George W. Bush was in tatters and candy was scattered across the lawn. "That's my girl," my mother said, squeezing my shoulders.

Sometimes I wonder what we are supposed to do with our memories. Sometimes I wonder what our memories are *for*. A latch slips and the past floods in, knocking us flat. We leave places and we don't leave places. Sometimes I imagine different versions of myself in all the different places I have ever lived, inching through time in parallel.

The flood vanishes without explanation. After four days of torrential rain, we wake up and look outside and find the streets empty, the asphalt pearled with water. The sky is ultramarine, cloudless. It reminds me of the sky in the English garden meditation, an unblemished blueness that carries an aura of the unreal. The sound of falling rain is gone, but it has not been replaced by other noises. I don't hear traffic or birds. "Goddamn," Arizona says, stepping onto the front porch. She's wearing a gray sweatsuit that belongs to my husband. We can only assume she lifted it from our bedroom closet when no one was looking. She pushes up the sleeves and looks around. "Feels like a trick to me, if you want to know the truth." Arizona is in the habit of telling people her version of the truth whether they want to know it or not. For example, when my niece asked Arizona if she thought her pet ghost might drown, Arizona told her that ghosts can't drown but what they can do is go wherever they want and so she struggled to see why a pet ghost would still be hanging around this waterlogged little town. On the Doppler, the sepia veil has vanished. It is as though a great mouth opened in the middle of the night and sucked up all the water. No one knows where the water went or when it will return. All we know is that we can go outside. We can walk the streets. We can search for my sister. All we know is that we have a window.

The meteorologists are now concerned that all this saturated earth will be susceptible to sinkholes. Already people are calling the city to report collapsed earth in roads, sidewalks, backyards, even though city ordinances do not like to call sinkholes what they actually are. They prefer to call them "depressions," and to seal them up with cold patches.

Two large sinkholes have opened up on the golf course of a nearby retirement community. One resident is quoted in the local paper as saying that, from a distance, the two craters resemble eyes.

Our cars are waterlogged, so my husband and I hurry down to the lake on foot. In the park, the missing-person signs have been swept away. All the tents have been uprooted. A massive, glistening sinkhole has torn open the park's center. On the edges, we find a few metal stakes, a drenched blanket, a blue tarp. The whole waterfront smells like an auditorium packed with decomposing fish. We are staggered by the stench. We yank our shirts up over our noses. The earth is covered in small, hard objects, amber-colored and shiny. I bend down and pick one up. "Is that a snail shell?" I say through my shirt. The cars parked along the lake are gone, except for the truck with DERMA, MISSISSIPPI painted along the side. "The preacher," my husband calls out. The passenger door is ajar. My husband pulls it open and water gushes out, drenching our sneakers. We find the bike man riding along the running path, no white dog in sight. He's wearing a black gas mask. "This smell feels deadly," he says when he stops. He explains that the dog got spooked by the incoming storm and bolted. The moment the water receded, he started riding around town, looking and looking. I think about seeing that tree full of cats. I think about how dogs can't climb. I think

about how the problem with running is that, once we get going, it can be hard to stop.

Later, on the news, we learn that millions of *Viviparus
georgianus*—banded mystery snails—were hauled ashore by
the storm and left stranded on land. They are called "mystery
snails" because the females somehow manage to give birth to
fully developed juvenile snails and then—quite mysteriously—
disappear. The mass death of snails is the source of the stench.
The meteorologist interviews a zoologist who specializes in
invertebrates. When the meteorologist asks why the snails
didn't find their way back to the water, the zoologist replies,
"Probably the snails hid in their shells and waited for condi-
tions to improve, but they never did." The meteorologist nods,
says he can relate.

There is an eeriness to this town, post-flood. My sister has
been missing for four days, and I wake each morning seasick
with dread, fingernails sunk into my pillow. All the cats have
vanished. My mother's house is even more tilted than before;
the wall hangings in the living room are skewed to hard angles. Parts of I-4 have been washed away, halting the Ultimate
Improvement Project. On the southeast coast, the ocean has
retreated. The meteorologist says this is called "reverse storm
surge," though normally it's not so dramatic, more like a low

tide. In Surfside, in Miami Beach, the water has been sucked back so powerfully it looks like the ocean has been replaced by a desert. I imagine the famous author, the assistants, looking out their windows and seeing a beige field, flat and firm enough for a person to walk across, in the direction of the now-faraway shoreline, violet and roiling in the distance. I can't help but feel that the water is just hiding out somewhere, waiting to launch another attack. I look upon all water with suspicion now: the cool stream that gushes from the faucet in my mother's kitchen, the warm, metallic dribble that comes from the mouths of water fountains, the immense and placid lake. When a wind passes over the surface the water quivers in a strange sort of way and I think about all those other worlds churning just beneath.

When my father still had ESP—before he fell down the stairs and broke his shoulder, before that portal closed—he had an uncanny ability to predict the weather. He would leave the house on a sunny morning in a rain jacket—on a day that was predicted to bring not a drop of water—and two hours later it would be apparent why. According to my mother, my father had no control over when his precognition arrived—he was not clairvoyant at all times, and it was not a skill he believed he could cultivate—but when it came the feeling was unmistakable. His left index finger trembled. His head felt like it was being pinched by a great claw. Apart from the weather, his ESP largely concerned his own affairs.

Once, he had plans to buy an investment property with a colleague from his law firm. At the last moment, he tore up the contracts. He'd been visited by a premonition about sitting down to do business with his colleague's wife, whom he regarded as difficult. Two weeks later, his colleague—who had just finished business in New York City and was bound for Miami Beach—perished when Eastern Airlines Flight 401 crashed into the Everglades.

In the aftermath of the Eastern Airlines crash, intact parts of the downed L-1011 were fitted onto other planes. All over the Everglades, for years to come, people reported seeing shadowy figures clinging to the exterior of passing Eastern Airlines flights. Ground crews spotted two spectral men sitting on the wings and talking. They were believed to be the captain and the first officer who perished in the crash. The ghost sightings persisted to such a degree that Eastern Airlines eventually removed all the salvaged parts from their aircraft, despite publicly denying the allegations that ghosts were hitching rides on their planes.

My brother-in-law organizes a search party. We congregate in my mother's yard. My brother-in-law holds a clipboard, checks names off a list. He's wearing his work uniform, khaki pants and a black polo shirt. He was ordered back to the factory the moment the floodwaters retreated; unimaginable disaster might ensue, his supervisor told him, if the making of labels was further disturbed. In addition to our family, he's managed to gather a co-worker from my sister's insurance company and a co-worker from the factory and a few neighbors, including Arizona, who is still wearing my husband's sweatsuit. After the flood vanished, she told us, she planned to return to her cousin's house, to see what could be salvaged, but she keeps appearing at my mother's place at the strangest times. I've found her wandering the front yard at six in the morning in a light mist. I've found her sniffing sheets of fabric softener in the laundry room. Meanwhile, I have started carrying a small spiral-top notepad and a black pen with me. I am in need of a new system for processing reality. The moment I see my brother-in-law's co-worker I know he belongs to the night shift. He has a pale, squishy body, ill-fitting pants, metal aviator eyeglasses. He drives a large white van, useful because we can all fit inside. We decide to start with the woods my sister called me from. Her last known location. The wilderness. My husband stays behind with my niece; everyone else rides out in the van. I see tents huddled together in parking lots, crooked billboards, sinkholes lying in wait like ravenous mouths. Before long, we are swallowed by a blue dusk. My brother-in-law's co-worker plays a tape of what sounds like muffled screaming. "It's a recording of whale communications," he explains. These anguished sounds run counter to how whales exist in my imagination, as serene giants of the sea. At the edge of the wilderness, I call my sister's name. I shine a small flashlight around and around. I look for the white sheen of the MIND'S EYE headset, even though I know anything my sister might have left behind in the wilderness has been washed away by the flood. The wooded area is smaller than I remember, and it doesn't take much time to cross from one tree line to the next. I discover a woman, crouched in a thicket of shadow. She is not part of our search party. She is holding a shovel; she is digging a hole. She's wearing a white T-shirt, denim coveralls, a red bandanna. "Are you okay?" I ask her. "Do you need help?" The woman pauses in her digging, leans against the shovel. Her T-shirt is soaked in sweat. "I'm looking for someone," she says. Just then I hear voices calling my name. Back in the van, I sit in the passenger seat, next to the factory co-worker. My mother is behind me, in a white button-down shirt and tan pants stuffed into muck boots. "I found something!" Arizona shouts from the back. She passes her discovery forward. One person after another holds out their hands, stares down with reverence. "What is it?" I call out. "What is it?" When the item finally reaches the front I see that it's an enormous tooth. My mother gazes at the tooth for a very long time. The tendons in her neck tighten like pulled strings. "Do you want to hold it?" my mother finally asks, with surprising tenderness. The tooth is actually several teeth, all fused together, sepia-colored and smooth to the touch. My hands drop under the weight. The teeth are far too big to have belonged to a bear or a panther. "It's a megalodon," the factory co-worker says. "Or maybe it's a mastodon. One of those." Turns out he's an amateur archaeologist. Or maybe, he says, this is the tooth of a massive shark—bigger than a great white—that has been extinct for several million years. From the back of the van, Arizona explains that the earth communicates with her through vibrations and when she was walking in the woods she felt a vibration so strong she was pitched forward, onto her hands and knees, and found herself staring at the giant tooth, half-buried in the dirt. She'd had a feeling that something ancient was trying to surface.

"Do you have any ChapStick?" the factory co-worker asks me on the way home. I covertly slip my hand under my shirt and slide two fingers into my belly button. I pull out the ChapStick and pass it to him. "This ChapStick is the perfect temperature," he says as he spreads it across his lips. On the way home, we pass an ancient Oldsmobile Cutlass, orange and boatlike, missing its rearview mirrors, with a bumper sticker that reads I DONATE MY PLASMA. At an intersection, we pass a camper stationed on the edge of a vacant lot, the windows covered by signs imploring us to HONK FOR JESUS. We drive through a symphony of horns.

At my mother's house, Arizona tucks the tooth under her arm like a loaf of bread and races off into the night. My brother-in-law trudges upstairs to put my niece to bed, where she will demand a story. Her current favorite is *The Tale of Samuel Whiskers*, about a kitten who accidentally gets caught in a roll of dough and is nearly eaten alive. *What a thing it is to have an unruly family!* My mother starts rummaging around in a closet and emerges with an electric typewriter. I have gauzy childhood memories of her sitting at the kitchen table and writing reports on this typewriter. Now she carries it over to the sofa and begins clacking away. My husband, exhausted from hearing about my niece's pet ghost, collapses into bed. In the attic bedroom, I put on the MIND'S EYE, stretch out on the floor, and enter the English garden. Everything is exactly as it was before. The spotless sky. The gleaming path. The velvet feel of the petals. The perfumed air. It is a relief, to visit a world where nothing seems to happen, a reality that cannot be disturbed, that remains untouched by catastrophe. I return to the ivy-covered wall. I kneel on the ground and stare hard at the trembling leaves. I feel certain there is something behind the ivy. I raise my hand, as though in greeting; a vibration ripples across my palm. The air quivers. I feel like I'm on the edge of a force field. *Touch*, I think. I thrust my hand into the cold, stiff leaves. My fingers are sucked deep into the bush; my cheek is shoved against the bramble. Something is trying to pull me inside. I yank my hand out, stagger backward. A dark static rains down. I blink and I'm returned to the beginning of the meditation, standing in front of the open garden gate.

After I leave the English garden, a tingling sensation moves in waves across my skin. The air in the attic bedroom smells

faintly of flowers, as if some part of the meditation has tracked
me back into my world. I sit in the chair and slap the tops of
my thighs until I've returned to my body. I try to make sense
of what was behind the ivy and what that presence wanted
from me. I glimpse a large, shadowed shape crouched in
the corner and think at first that I am experiencing a minor
hallucination, but then the shape quivers and sniffs and I
realize it's a person. I tilt the lamplight toward the corner
and there's Arizona, bundled up in a pink quilt that belongs
to my niece. "How did you even get up here?" I ask her. "I
practice polyphasic sleep," she replies. "That means I sleep for
three hours, stay awake for two, and then sleep for three more.
Polyphasic sleeping is much closer to how animals sleep in
the wild." She sheds the quilt, unfolds her body. She has a
build that is slight yet imposing. When she roots herself in
place she looks sinewy and solid, hard to move. In the soft
night of the room, her nose ring shimmers. "You should be
careful with that thing." She points at the white headset on
the desk. She has hands like a child's, with short fingers and
small palms. "I used the one they gave us during the pandemic, and boy, did it fuck me up." One strange thing about
this neighbor is that she told us the house swap with her
cousin started in January, but I can't remember ever seeing
her around until the flood. I watch her climb down the attic staircase, the pink quilt wrapped around her shoulders.
I listen to the patter of her footsteps moving through the
house. The house with which she is, by now, disconcertingly
familiar. I look out the window, where the streets are empty

and dry, until I see her slip away from my mother's property and run out into the darkness, the quilt flapping like a cape.

At the Institute, I used to have dreams about digging. In these dreams, I would claw at the cold hard floors until my nails were broken and bloodied. Eventually I would strike earth. At first, the earth would be as unyielding as stone, but I would keep going until I hit something soft. Then I would wake in bed, alone in a dark room. I would sit up and sniff my fingertips. I would lie back down, defeated, and wait for the night shift orderly to come check on me. Tonight, in bed with my husband and dog, I dream once again about digging, only this time I'm in the wilderness where my sister was last seen, sinking my hands into the soil. Here, the earth is supple. It gives and it gives and soon it is as though I have made a large hole in a great ceiling and now I am looking down into a room from another world. I slide into that room and there I find familiar people—my husband, my sister, my brother-in-law, my dog, my niece—but everyone is wearing someone else's face. My husband is wearing my sister's face and my mother is wearing my brother-in-law's face and my dog is wearing my niece's face and vice versa. I sit bolt upright, sweat trickling down my throat. I check the stubbled face of my husband, who is sound asleep beside me, and the golden, whiskered face of my dog. I check my belly button, still a small tunnel. My mouth is hot and dry. I go downstairs for a glass of water. In the living room, my mother's electric typewriter sits on the coffee table, next to a stack of paper with a yellow sticky note on top. The note reads MANIFESTO. At the kitchen sink, I sip water from a coffee mug and look out the window. The darkness appears liquid. The air is moving in a strange way. Like it is trying to turn into something solid. To make a shape. I assume it's Arizona roaming around in my mother's yard. Someone has got to tell this woman to stop skulking around like a lunatic. I go outside. I walk softly across the grass. I see a figure rolling around on the earth. "Hello?" I call out. The figure leaps up. In the light cast by the kitchen, I can make out my sister's face. I run to her. I grab her by the shoulders. Her hair is wet and clinging to her skull. Her long cheeks are streaked with dirt. The white MIND'S EYE headset is sliding around on her neck. "Where have you been?" I shout. "Where did you come from?" My sister looks watery, dazed. "I was attempting to travel from one world to another," she tells me, blinking wildly. "And somehow I ended up back here."

My sister wants to go for a drive. The night is hot and quiet. "What happened here?" She presses a hand to the passenger window. She stares out at the field that used to be filled with tents, missing-person signs. The landscape has been transformed into something desolate and unrecognizable. "We had a Major Weather Event," I tell her. I want to fling my arms around my sister and cling like a homesick child. She nods. She clutches the white headset in her lap. Dirt is packed under her fingernails. Her long hair looks like it's been oiled. She smells of sweat, mineral, fresh earth. She keeps saying the word "portal." She keeps saying "MIND'S EYE." She keeps putting these words together in the same sentence. As in: *MIND'S EYE is filled with portals.* I listen to the swift cadence of her voice. I feel like I am being carried away by whitewater rapids. I try to hold on. I dock the car by the lake. At this hour, the body of water is as smooth and black as a gemstone. I take out my notebook and write down what my sister is telling me, about how our father kept appearing in the English garden and saying *There is something I want you to do*, about how he wanted her to enter one of these portals and access another reality. The directives of the dead are very powerful, so she obeyed his instructions and emerged in a sleeping pod at Miami International Airport. She felt light-headed, peculiar, but nevertheless managed to leave the airport in a rental car. "How do you know that's what happened?" I ask her. "How can you be sure?" She tells me that, on Route 1, she passed a digital billboard displaying the faces of people who had perished during the pandemic. When she saw her own face on the billboard, enormous and shimmering, she almost drove the rental car off the road.

"Look here." She reaches into her bra and takes out a small square photo. "I found this after Dad told me to get a certain photo album out of my attic. This picture was stuck behind one of us on Easter in 1989. We both had the most hideous haircuts." She hands over the photo. I stare down at two adult women in white tennis dresses. Identical twins. They have shoulder-length auburn hair, flipped out at the ends, and round hazel eyes. They look thin lipped, serious. "Remember Mom's favorite bad-dad story?" she says. "About the phone call she got right after her honeymoon? From the woman who was pregnant with twins?" I begin to sort their features into two piles: the twins have our father's high forehead and hazel eyes and long straight fingers. The red hair and the thin lips belong to someone else. "I was supposed to find the twins, but I failed," my sister says. "I let everyone down. I freaked, after I saw my big dead face on that billboard." She locked herself in the rental car. She jammed the headset back on. She tore through the English garden and the next thing she knew she'd landed in our mother's backyard.

In my early days at the Institute, I tried to convince myself that I had accidentally fallen through a wormhole and into a different reality. Sometimes, at night, I would get out of bed and walk around my room. I would press both my hands against different spots on the wall and imagine all those hard materials yielding to my touch. I would imagine plummeting through some other dimension until I found my way back to the world I once belonged to. These were the kinds of notions that preoccupied me when I was out of my mind. In the car, I feel terrified by the things I am writing down, by the hard break my sister seems to have made from reality. I close the notebook and cap the pen. "If these twins really exist," I say, "then why can't we just go find them in this world?" My sister turns to me. In the night, her eyes are such a rich shade of gold they appear yellow. Like two little moons. Her expression is heavy with tenderness and pity. "Because the twins died in the pandemic," she says. In this other world, she claims, the twins survive the pandemic but die six months later, when their neighborhood floods. What our father wants is for her—for us—to find the twins in their world and bring them back here. To save them. "Dad seems to have a lot of regrets, now that he's dead," my sister says. "There are certain things he's trying to make right."

"Of course, I can't tell anyone else what really happened." She taps her nails against the car window. "They'll think I've snapped." I am careful to not agree or disagree. I do not tell my sister that I'm scared the wilderness has finally come for her. I imagine a vine snaking around her ankle and dragging her into the trees. "I'll tell everyone I had a nervous collapse," my sister goes on. "A midlife crisis. An existential meltdown. Which would only be a half lie. I'm pretty sure I've been having an existential meltdown for years."

"What's this?" my sister asks, back at our mother's house. She's standing in the living room, pointing down at the stack of paper with the MANIFESTO sticky note. She sits on the edge of the couch and begins to sift through the pages. I watch her shoulders hike up to her ears. "I can't even deal with this bullshit right now," she says, standing with her fists clenched. "Where's my family?" I point at the stairs and she storms up to the second floor. I stand at the foot of the stairs and listen to the door crack open. A wave of adult voices, low and then loud, and then the wild pitch of my niece, bellowing for her mother. I go to the pages on the coffee table, curious to see what upset my sister. The more I read the more it becomes clear that my mother is now an advocate for the voluntary human extinction movement. *The problem with every utopia*, my mother writes, *is that they are designed for people. When in fact there cannot be a utopia with people in it. When in fact we are the problem.*

In the middle of the night, the neighborhood is shaken awake by a major explosion. In the morning, we learn that the culprit is a ruptured gas line. Some claim it was an accident. Others declare it an act of terrorism. A woman who lives down the street looked out her window and saw a great orange fireball in the sky. She thought it was a massive asteroid and that she was seconds away from annihilation. She dropped to her knees from a heart attack right then and there. *It was like something out of that movie with Bruce Willis*, she tells a newspaper reporter from her hospital bed.

. . .

Did anyone else hear those screams outside? a woman posts on Nextdoor. *Sounded like the screams of several hundred (thousand??) dying souls or something?! I'm terrified lol.*

A man on Nextdoor asks if anyone can recommend a good paranormal investigator. The man has lived alongside a presence in his house for a long time, but the presence never caused a disturbance. At the most, he would occasionally smell someone cooking breakfast in the kitchen in the middle of the night. Lately, he has been waking up with tiny crosses scratched into his legs. Once, he was even pinned to the bed and then thrown across the room. He is not sure if he has done something to upset the presence, or if the presence has been usurped by one that is far more hostile.

A Florida man plows his Dodge Challenger into a strip mall, decimating a casket retailer and an H&R Block. The Florida man says that he has reason to believe a portal to another world exists in the wall that divides these two businesses and if he drove into this wall, at top speed, he would access the ability to travel through time.

. . .

In the local paper, I come across an ad for an informational meeting about the VOLUNTARY HUMAN EXTINCTION MOVEMENT, to be held tomorrow at my mother's house.

At the Institute, I became acquainted with a woman named Susan Virtue. She was in her mid-thirties and she moved around the place with the familiarity of a regular at her favorite bar. She wore her sandy hair in a bob and her skin had an orange tint because, before being admitted, she'd been on a diet that consisted exclusively of carrots. Boiled carrots, pickled carrots, baby carrots, and so on. "I never felt so wonderful," she claimed, though all this wonder had not been enough to stop her from taking a flier from the top of her apartment building. Her left arm was still in a cast, which she invited everyone to sign. Some people came and went from the wilderness, but Susan Virtue lived there. Before I was discharged, she gave me a business card with her information. I sent her a few messages through the years, like a photo from a u-pick carrot farm in north Florida. In the picture, I'm holding a dirt-clodded bundle of carrots by their green tendrils. Several years ago, I got an email from Susan Virtue. She was living in New York City. She needed to get to Florida but she had developed a phobia of flying, and she wanted to know if I would be willing to travel with her. As it happened, I had plans to visit for the birth of my niece. I gave her my information, assumed nothing would come of it, but a few days later she forwarded me an itinerary for the same flight. She even got the seat next to me. I told no one about this curious turn of events. Well, no one except my dog. *I'm going to be reunited with Susan Virtue*, I whispered into his silky ear. It was a shock to see her at the airport. Her blond hair had grown long and heavy. She walked with a slight limp. On the plane, she asked what I was doing with myself and I told her I had become a writer. Why not take some liberties. She was traveling to Florida to be admitted to a clinic in Naples. Her mother had died some years ago, leaving her a good bit of money, so she could check herself into whatever kind of clinic she wanted. She told me that Florida had her favorite psychiatric facilities in the country. "Well, not where we were," she clarified. "I'm talking yoga, gourmet food, sunshine." The strangest part of this whole journey was that Susan Virtue did not seem afraid of flying. She did not shudder when the plane was batted around by turbulence or when the seat belt sign glowed an evil red. "Am I different than you remember?" I asked her. She twisted around in her seat and squinted at me. "What I remember is someone who barely spoke. Like there was a wall of silence between you and everyone else. You always looked lost, even when you were just outside your room. Oh! And I remember your father coming to see you. What a charmer! You could tell from a mile away." At the time, my father was still alive; I promised to pass on Susan Virtue's regards. When we landed in Orlando, I asked if someone from the clinic was coming to collect her, or if she would rent a car. She began to list all the things she needed to do before she even considered leaving the airport. She needed to eat at the Chipotle; use the restroom in Terminal C because international terminals have the cleanest toilets; get a ten-minute massage. Maybe she would even check into the airport hotel for a night. "Being a patient is serious business," she said. "I have to prepare." I wondered if preparation meant exercising every choice available until you were so exhausted that it would be a relief to have your choices taken away. By then I understood that there wasn't an important or mysterious motivation behind Susan Virtue's contacting me; I had just been another choice she could exercise. "The last time I was on this thing I saw a UFO," she said as we boarded the people mover. "I showed it to the man next to me and he said it was an optical illusion. That altitude can make things in the sky look different. I didn't buy it, but I played along. Some events are too big to even acknowledge."

"Dad is back," my sister whispers through the backyard fence. "He's back and he's not happy at all." There is a small gap between the wood slats; I can make out the golden flicker of her eyes. "I thought you were swearing off MIND'S EYE," I say. The sun beats down. My heartbeat is a little band of thunder inside my chest. "It's not as easy as you make it out to be," my sister replies, her voice low and pleading. "I know how this sounds, but it's like we're in a relationship, me and this device." When I ask her what she means by relationship, she says, "It calls out to me." I want to climb over to her side of the yard, clutch her shoulders, and shake. "Well, I don't

know what Dad expects us to do," I say. "I don't know either,"
she replies. "But he certainly expects us to do something."
Just then my sister gasps. "I think Mom's house is about to be
burgled." I look over my shoulder and catch Arizona slipping
through a downstairs window in the gray sweatsuit she stole
from my husband. "That's just Arizona," I tell her. "We found
her during the flood." Next my sister asks, "But who are all
those other people?" I turn around and see a stream of people
filing into the yard. This is the day of our mother's meeting.

My sister refuses to attend the meeting, as she objects to the
premise of voluntary human extinction, but my husband and
I are curious. We watch from the threshold of the kitchen.
There are maybe a dozen people in the living room. Some I
recognize from around town; others are strangers. My mother
spends the majority of the meeting reading her manifesto.
She sits in a large red armchair, positioned in the center of
the living room. Arizona has volunteered to be her assistant;
she stands by my mother and hands her one page after the
next. As I listen, I wonder if the manifesto is like a portal for
my mother. To write it was to build a door. Now she is opening that door and stepping through to the other side. After
my mother finishes reading a page, she releases the paper,
lets it drift down to the floor. I find it hard to argue with
some of her ideas. After all, it takes a disposable diaper more
than four centuries to biodegrade in a landfill. "We have all
been trying to outrun the inevitable reality," my mother says,

lifting a page. "Everything is a distraction from the most important thing."

That night, in the attic room, I attempt to create an outline of the book I intend to write, so I can offer the assistants some evidence that I am up to the task. I research "how to outline a novel." Maybe it was a bad idea, to attempt to write about the Institute, and I need a change of direction. According to one website, I should complete the following sentence: [Character] **must** [do something] **in order to** [stakes] **or else** [consequences].

> [Protagonist] **must** [solve the mystery of whatever it is that's going on] **in order to** [?] **or else** [?].

> [Protagonist] **must** [?] **in order to** [?] **or else** [her sister will be lost to the wilderness].

> [Protagonist] **must** [?] **in order to** [?] **or else** [she will never see her father again].

At two in the morning, *Season of Death* sails off the desk like it's been thrown. The air turns thin and cool. I am powerfully relieved to have a reason to stand up from my desk, to break away from this terrible exercise. "Dad?" I call out. "Was that you?" I pick up *Season of Death*. The book has finally dried since I rescued it during the Major Weather Event. The paper is stiff and some of the pages are stuck together, but the story is still legible.

In *Season of Death*, another grizzled-yet-noble detective participates in an experimental project conducted by a Miami-based tech company. The detective travels back to the seventies to prevent the death of his mother, who was murdered by a serial killer when the detective was a child. But then, because the serial killer never murders the detective's mother, and is thus never arrested and jailed, he goes on a killing spree in the present timeline. This turns out to be the tech company's plan all along: they wanted to eliminate a rival CEO—who happens to be the serial killer's exact physical type—and decided this was the way to commit the perfect crime.

The assistants are right, I think, as I pull apart the pages. Despite the outlandish plot, the famous author's earlier style is less blunt, less sensationalist, less absurd. There are descriptions that alight in the mind's eye; there are similes. In the opening chapter there is even an em dash. Not a single character says *everything is not as it seems* even though everything is *not* as it seems. There is still foreshadowing that hangs like a great shadow over the end of each chapter. I can detect evidence of the writer the famous author would become, in other words, just as I can see why the assistants steered me away from the early works. They would have given me too much hope. They would have encouraged me to believe that we were real writers, here to do real writing. That we had come together to tell a story.

In chapter three, I learn that the Miami-based tech company is called ELECTRA. Even though the ELECTRA that I know, the ELECTRA that belongs to this world, was founded a decade after this book was written.

Are you up, I text my sister. *I think I've found a clue.*

I open an upstairs window and hurl *Season of Death* over my mother's fence and into my sister's backyard. I have long believed that there is something wrong with ELECTRA, but it never occurred to me that the famous author might be involved. There is a passage in *Principles of Plot* that discusses the moment in the story where the stakes get raised, where the protagonist stands on the threshold of a radically new understanding. Like Susan Virtue I must now prepare. I take a shower. I slide a bar of soap into the tunnel that has emerged behind my belly button and give it a good clean. I get dressed and go downstairs and sit on the edge of the couch.

· · ·

Well shit, my sister texts, just before dawn. *I think we need to go talk to your boss.*

Several days ago my husband gave me a page of notes from his book about pilgrimages.

> *Pilgrims were people wondering, wondering.*
> *Pilgrims were people who loved a good riddle.*
> *Pilgrims were people who carried knives but who rarely found use for them.*
> *When we are denied a story, a light goes off.*

I read his notes over three times in a row. Then I roll the page into a tiny scroll and slip it inside my belly button.

Recently my husband told me that he had lost his way with the book he was writing, so much so that it had turned into something else.

The Institute

To get to Palm Beach we must follow a series of numbers: the 417 to the 528 to I-95. My sister drives her white SUV, with a dirty windshield and Cheerios smashed into the floor mats. On the news, we've heard that the roads around Palm City are still washed out. We're not certain what we will find as we drive south, but we will go as far as we can. My sister leans forward in her seat, curls her long fingers around the wheel. When we see signs for Melbourne, I ask if she remembers the Giant Orange. I want to direct her attention back to the real world. "One of the most disastrous outings in our family history," she replies, shaking her head. The orange is made from painted steel and concrete, built in the sixties, on a sparse patch of grass. It stands fifteen feet tall, with a bright green stem and leaves. When it was first built, the chamber of commerce served orange juice to tourists through a little front window on Saturday afternoons. Once, when we were children, we were driving to the beach and our parents got into a shrieking argument. They pulled over at the Giant Orange; our mother ran around the side, opened the door in the back, darted in, and bolted the lock. Our father circled the orange. He pounded his fists against the round metal sides. Finally he turned to us, car keys clenched in his large hand, and said, "We'll show her." We went to the beach and spent two unsettled hours splashing around in the ocean. After a young boy was nearly carried away by a riptide, my father decided it was time to go; by then the whole excursion felt cursed. When we returned to the Giant Orange, the door was hanging open, our mother gone. We searched the area in a sweaty panic. Finally, we drove home. Our father did not speak or turn on the radio. On the 520, he picked up a hitchhiker, a young man in denim shorts and aviator sunglasses. The hitchhiker told us he'd just finished a stint at a cannery in Del Ray Beach and was making his way north. He had small callused hands and a musical laugh. "In another life, I was a repo man," he said. "Once I had to repossess a houseboat where a couple had been raising ferrets. That was it for me. All that ferret shit, man. I was done." We left the ex–repo man at a gas station. At home, we found our mother waiting on the front porch, drinking a glass of white wine. She raised the glass as my father lumbered out of the car, head hung, outfoxed. Later, we would learn that our mother phoned a friend who lived near Melbourne and got a ride. Our parents were like that for the entirety of their marriage, always plotting against each other.

"What did you see inside the orange?" I asked my mother a few days after this incident. "A reflection," my mother replied. I asked her how that was possible—did the giant orange have mirrors inside?—but she refused to elaborate.

. . .

My sister exits the highway, starts following signs for the Giant Orange. "This could be the perfect place." She turns into the parking lot. "The perfect place for what?" I ask. The parking lot is empty. Ahead the orange looks like a lonely little planet, trapped behind a chain-link fence. The paint has faded and the stem appears smaller, as though it is sinking down into the dome. My sister gets out of the car and opens the trunk. She returns holding our white MIND'S EYE headsets. "Enough of this," I tell her. I pound my fists against my thighs. She hops into the car and slides the headset on. She reclines her seat. "When you get to the ivy keep going," my sister tells me. "It helps to get a running start."

In the English garden, I decide to indulge my sister's fantasies. Perhaps this indulgence is the only way to bring her back down to the earth. I stare down the path at the wall of ivy and the distant red glint of the apple orchard. *Run*, I think. I imagine how my husband looks when he runs; I bow my head and pump my arms. It's like racing into a giant wave, the way it feels solid at first, and then breaks and crashes, dragging me into a dimension of overwhelming sensation and sound.

I push up my headset. I'm a little breathless, a little warm. I look left and then right. My neck cracks. The world around appears unchanged. We're still in my sister's car. Blue sky, a parking lot, a giant orange behind a chain-link fence. "See?"

I tell her. "Nothing happened." She starts the car and turns in the direction of the highway. "We'll see about that," she replies. I consider how best to tell my sister that she is operating under a delusion. *You are not yourself right now.* That was what people kept saying to me when I had a head full of bees and wanted to kill the hive. I never understood what they meant by that, because I had never before felt myself so powerfully. The self inside me was like a wildfire: glowering, ravenous. I was being eaten alive by self. Back then I sincerely felt like I was getting to the bottom of something.

You are not where you think you are. That could be one way to begin.

When the exit signs for Fort Lauderdale start to loom, I slip my hand under my shirt and push my entire fist into my belly button. I concentrate on the cutting pressure of my knuckles, the sensation of holding tight to something that can barely be contained. My sister hunches over the wheel and steps on the gas. "We need to make another stop," she tells me, and this time I know exactly where she's headed. She flies down an exit ramp and soon we're in the parking lot of a municipal building. Seventies brutalist, faux brick and tan siding, a trio of weather-beaten palm trees in a gravel pool, a centerpiece in the circular entrance. A person would be shocked to know what could go on in such an ordinary-looking place. "Is this right?" my sister asks. "Is this what you remember?" I get out of the car. I move toward the building in slow, dazed steps. I am astonished by what I find. The Institute has been abandoned. The windows are boarded up. The palm trees are dead, the fronds brown and drooping. The front door is padlocked. This is not a recent closure. I can tell from the green vines that have overtaken a ground-floor window. Yet I know for a fact that the Institute is still in operation. On occasion, I still survey the building on Street View. Just last month I got an email from the Institute, inviting me to attend their annual Reunion Day. "No," I tell her. "This is all wrong." At the same time, some things are right, like the architecture and the faint smell of burning rubber in the parking lot. "I'm sorry for bringing you back here," my sister says. "But I needed, if you will, a reality check. A point of comparison. I needed to see if we're still in our world, or if we are actually someplace else."

I walk around to the side of the building, where I find one familiar detail: a long rectangular window, made of frosted glass. The panes are cloudy and cracked, but in the parking lot I remember this window as it used to be. That window belonged to the staff room, off limits for patients, but on occasion the door was left ajar. In the late afternoon, I would pass by in the hallway and glimpse the night shift orderly taking a nap on a cot, or just standing in the center of the room with a cup of coffee, moving a red plastic stirrer around in very slow circles.

At the Institute, plenty of people were nice enough to me, but it was always in the service of wanting me to do something. Every interaction was laced with agenda. The friendliness was a mask that fell the moment I refused to swallow a pill or to crochet a winter cap in silence. Never mind that there was no need for winter caps in Florida. So I learned how to perform. I learned how to fake everything. In anger work, I screamed at a pitch that made my tonsils vibrate. I thrashed the pillows with the foam bat. I let Cindy hold me in the aftermath, wipe the fake tears from my steaming cheeks. It was like the psychiatric patient's version of the orgasm scene in *When Harry Met Sally*. Now I think the night shift orderly was faking everything too. I think that is what must have drawn us toward each other: the stench of each other's grift. I think the night shift orderly came to work at the Institute because he was a dangerous person, but he had learned to keep his danger under cover. The patients—his charges during the midnight hours—were dangerous people too, but we had let our danger out into the open and that was why we were here. I think he wanted to be around people like us, to study us, to see where we had gone wrong. To see what we were really like when we thought no one was looking.

· · ·

By the time the night shift orderly started asking me for
OED words of the day I could have been at the Institute for
a week or a month or a year. The clock had turned liquid,
inscrutable.

Hagfish. Sung-through. Obsequious. Iridic. Hithermost. Sulcus. Lucernal. Rhynchodont. Unigenous. Interlucation. Triplopia. Distelfink.

The challenge was to use the word of the day correctly in a
sentence. I started to spend a lot of time studying the dictionary, in hopes of stumping him, but the night shift orderly
seemed to be in possession of a vast vocabulary. Sometimes
he was right—*I suffer from triplopia*; *Cindy is so obsequious
around the director*—and sometimes he was wrong. *Every
night I am visited by a sulcus.* (*I think you mean succubus.*) Or
half-wrong. *You look so lucernal today.*

It was during these exchanges that I became a writer. I
thought, at first, that we were engaging in a cut-and-dried
exercise. The night shift orderly would use the word either
correctly or incorrectly. Over time, I began to understand
how flexible language could be. How ambiguous, how porous,
how dense. Like a bucket without a bottom. Still, that bottomless bucket could hold the deepest feelings and the most

inexpressible realities. A word could be wrong and somehow the meaning could still be right. For example, on the night he called me "lucernal" my hair had recently been cut into a bob that did indeed resemble a triangular lampshade.

Fuck the rules, language said to me, *and find the truth*.

One night the word was "crepuscular," and the orderly said, *The light will be crepuscular soon* and then he asked me if I wanted to get out of here.

In the moment, I felt like my prayers had been answered, even though I had not technically been praying. Just wishing very hard. There was nothing of mine in the room and so there was nothing to take with me. I had no shoes. I just put on my thickest socks and followed the night shift orderly down the shadowed hall.

He turned off his flashlight. He took my hand and led me down a stairwell. Even now I can still hear the light rain of our footsteps. Still feel the dry heat of his skin. He whispered that he knew how to leave the Institute without passing through the gaze of a security camera. All I had to do was keep following him. I had been out of reality—out of

LAURA VAN DEN BERG

time—for so long that I felt like we were playing a game and that before we actually left the building we would be discovered by some higher authority.

Which did not happen. All the higher authorities must have been sleeping soundly.

Outside I remembered that I was still in Florida. The air was so wet and so sweet. The spiked green heads of palm trees shuddered in a sea breeze. The night shift orderly had parked his car not in the main lot, but on an unlit street. He held the passenger door open for me. He buckled my seat belt. He started the car and drove away without turning on the headlights. In fact, he did not switch them on until we were approaching the highway. "How do I look?" I asked him when we were paused at a stoplight. He studied me, one hand on the steering wheel and the other on the gearshift. *Less lucernal than you used to*, he replied.

I assumed that he was going to take me to where he lived, but that is not what happened. He kept driving and driving. Through the passenger window I watched the sky darken, from a midnight blue to a dense jet black. I watched the edges of the clouds come into focus. *Now this is crepuscular light*, the night shift orderly said as we crossed our first state line, from Florida into Mississippi.

I have not yet described the night shift orderly's face, because I sincerely cannot remember it. His features are something my memory has blotted out, without my consent. I can see the outline of his body, short but strong, muscular arms and shoulders. I can see the dirty-blond waves of hair. When I try and hone in on his face, however, there is only a flat and featureless oval of light. In my imagination I have replaced his face with Mark Wahlberg's, even though I suspect that comparison only flatters the night shift orderly. Sometimes I worry that I could pass him on the street and have no idea who he was.

Unless, that is, he struck up a conversation, because I will never forget the sound of his voice.

In the parking lot of a service station, the night shift orderly pulled out a pair of glasses from the glove compartment and asked me to put them on. They had large rectangular frames—like what a woman with big hair in the seventies might have worn—and were made of champagne-colored acetate. The lenses were smudged. They felt warm on my face. The person to whom the lenses had been prescribed must have been half-blind, because they fuzzed the landscape, rounded all the shapes, and dimmed the lights. When I asked him why he wanted me to wear these glasses he told me that they helped him to remember someone who mattered to him but who was no longer in his life.

We kept driving. Sometimes I would slide the glasses down and glimpse a road sign—we were in Gulfport, we were in Houston—and the night shift orderly would lean over and flick me on the arm. A sharp little sting.

At service stations, there were other things the night shift orderly asked me to wear. A pair of vintage blue plastic cluster clip earrings. They were heavy and tugged on my earlobes. A plain gold signet ring, to be worn on my right hand. A V-neck sweater, made of an itchy baby-blue wool. A black wig that smelled of mothballs. Everything emerged from the glove compartment, except for the wig, which came out of the trunk.

We are running away together, the night shift orderly whispered as we passed through Galveston. *Isn't that exciting?* To my astonishment, I felt only a deep drowsiness. At the last service station, I'd asked the orderly to bring me something hot to drink. The coffee had been thick with cream and it had not occurred to me that I was about to be drugged. In the car, I drifted in and out of sleep. I had a dream that there was a black cat in the back seat, clawing the seats and meowing. Each time the cat ripped a hole in the fabric, water spurted out.

We were nearly to Corpus Christi when the police lights loomed in the rearview, a small flicker that grew until it was all I could see behind us, a flashing wall of blue and red. *We're so close*, the orderly said, grasping my wrist. The next thing I knew an officer was pulling me out of the car and draping a silver thermal blanket over my shoulders. Even though it was hot outside, in South Texas. Later, I would learn that the night shift orderly had plans to cross the border into Mexico, where we would then disappear.

Would you believe that the whole time I hit the pillows during anger work I was thinking about clouds? I still can't believe that the average cumulus cloud weighs more than a million pounds.

My sister and I sit in the parking lot for a while, our backs to the Institute. I take some comfort in knowing that, in this reality at least, the place has been defeated. "Is it hard for you to be here?" My sister places a cool hand on my forearm. I nod. I feel like I am crying—my cheeks are burning hot, my chest quivering—but my face is dry. "Do you ever miss him?" she asks next, and I know she is talking about the night shift orderly.

Maybe a different version of my story goes like this. At the Institute, I learned how to perform. I learned how to fake everything. In anger work, I screamed at a pitch that made my tonsils vibrate. I thrashed the pillows with the foam bat. I let Cindy hold me in the aftermath, wipe the fake tears from my steaming cheeks. After ten months, I was told I would be discharged. On my last night, the word was "crepuscular." The night shift orderly said, *The light will be crepuscular soon*, and then he asked me if I wanted to get out of here. There was nothing of mine in the room and so there was nothing to take with me. I had no shoes. I just put on my thickest socks and followed the night shift orderly down the dark hall. The orderly led me up a stairwell and we sat on the flat roof, looking at the sky. I told him about a word I had recently discovered: *apterygial, adj. Destitute of fins, finless. See: snakes, eels. When I was a child I had an apterygial pet.* On the roof, the night shift orderly told me to not be too mad at my parents. When my father visited for the first time, he slipped the night shift orderly a twenty, asked him to keep an eye on me. "Everything is going to be okay," the night shift orderly said next. Then he leaned over and kissed me on the mouth. He held the back of my head with one hand, used the other to cup my breast. He pressed his tongue between my lips. He tasted like coffee, vanilla creamer, peppermint. "I've been wanting to do this for months," he whispered, his breath a little blowtorch on my neck. On the roof, I felt both alarmed and enthralled. I dug my fingernails into his shoulders. I felt something inside me wake up. By the time we pulled away from each other I had decided I was in love with him. Before I left the Institute, we exchanged numbers. I called the night shift orderly every time I thought about him, which amounted to several dozen times a day. Also, I wrote him letters. At first he answered some of these calls and then he stopped. After he stopped, I drove down to the Institute in the middle of the night and waited for him in the parking lot. When he emerged at dawn, he was not, to my surprise, pleased to see me. "You've got to stop this," he hissed as he brushed past. "I could lose my job." I did not know how to explain that I had been released into a world so bewildering that I felt like a canoe in a tsunami. It felt like an abduction, this period of time. It felt outlandish, improbable, to be kidnapped and held hostage by my own state of mind. Eventually the director of the Institute placed a call to my parents; my sister answered and pretended to be our mother. "You had better stop calling him," she said to me. So I stopped calling the night shift orderly. I went to outpatient therapy. I went to AA. I showed up to my college classes, especially if they had anything to do with books. I finished my degree. I fled north, into the arms of literature. I spent years and years imagining many different versions of this story, searching for the one that could match what it felt like to live it.

After we leave the Institute, my sister drives us over to the electronic billboard on Route 1. The memorial to the victims of the pandemic. The billboard is massive, the length of an airplane; it looms like a roadside attraction. We pull over onto the opposite shoulder. We get out and sit on the hood. We watch the faces change. Each dead face is huge and twinkling. On the billboard, my sister's teeth are big and white. They make me think of cliffs.

The White Pantsuits

The streets around Palm Beach look normal enough, wide and clean and manicured. The famous author lives in a neo-classical mansion on Ocean Boulevard; we were able to find photos online, courtesy of a gossip magazine. From the outside, the entire house is bone white except for blue marble columns. We stop outside a white guardhouse, where a man in a black suit and reflective sunglasses asks me who I am and what I think I'm doing here. I give him my name. He turns his back to us and speaks softly into a walkie-talkie. Seconds later, to my surprise, the boom barrier rises.

A woman in a white pantsuit opens the front door. She has the crimson lips and the cascading blond curls of a Hollywood starlet. The white pantsuit is spotless and perfectly pressed. The jacket is buttoned. The white hems of the pants fall just below the ankles, where they brush against the soft pink edges of suede kitten heels. The suit looks exactly like the one that Hillary Clinton wore on the campaign trail. If this woman is one of the assistants, she is not at all what I have imagined during our many correspondences. She waves me inside, where we stand together in a great atrium. There is no art or furniture, just soaring gold walls and a domed glass ceiling. "We've been expecting you," the woman in white says.

My sister and I follow the woman in white down a long hallway and into an office with French doors that look out on an interior courtyard. The courtyard has a three-tier iron fountain in the center, surrounded by curved hedges and orange birds-of-paradise. The office is filled with amber-colored bamboo furniture and thick carpets with intricate red-and-gold designs. It has the feel of a place where men retire to smoke cigars and drink scotch and discuss world affairs in tones that make it sound like they are the rulers of the universe. The woman in white sits across from us behind a bamboo-and-leather desk, her features softly illuminated by a gold lamp. She has deep-set blue eyes and a Roman nose and teeth that look a little too large in her mouth. "Why were you expecting her?" my sister wants to know. "We're all big fans," the woman in white replies. My sister cuts a glance at me, one eyebrow arched. When I ask the woman if she is an assistant, she replies, "We all started out as an assistant to someone. The problem is that most people stay assistants for-ever. They never learn how to take charge of their lives. How to lead." The walls are lined with bookshelves; all the books have linen spines. No glossy dust jackets, like the ones on the famous author's novels. I ask the woman in white if this room is where the famous author comes up with his ideas;

she tilts her head and smiles serenely. "We never discuss the details of the author's process. At all times we respect the privacy of creation. I'm sure you, of all people, can understand." I take out *Season of Death* and slide it across the table. "Oh, this old thing?" The woman in white peers down at the book. "It's practically an antique. The author moved on from this style a long time ago." She pushes *Season of Death* back in my direction with the tip of her index finger. "Nevertheless," I reply, "we need to know how he wrote that book."

The woman in white suggests a tour of the house. I can tell that she means to distract us from the purpose of our visit, but still my sister and I follow along. *Action leads to more action.* That's another tip I remember from *Principles of Plot.* We exit the office and move into the interior courtyard, where our voices are blunted by the soft rushing of the fountain. She shows us a small greenhouse with a collection of carnivorous plants. Venus flytraps, bladderworts, corkscrews, pitcher plants. "Carnivorous plants are one of the author's passions," she says, dropping a cricket into the yawning green mouth of a pitcher plant. "What the fuck is this place," my sister whispers under her breath. Next we find ourselves in a massive library with large tan reading chairs, white ladders to reach the highest shelves, and massive gold chandeliers. Then in a dining room with a long mahogany table, iron candlesticks, chairs with rams' heads carved into the wood backs, a boat-sized crystal chandelier. Eventually we wind up back in the atrium. We end where we began. "The author is away on a research trip," she says. "Please do come back another time." I ask the woman in white how long the author will be away and she replies that it's impossible to know. Sometimes these trips take weeks or even months. "The creative process is highly unpredictable." I brandish *Season of Death* once more. "All we want is a conversation," I tell the woman in white. "Enough of this bullshit." My sister steps forward. She threatens to enlist her entire community to review-bomb the famous author's latest book online. "I'm president of the gardening club and the neighborhood association. I know a lot of people." The woman in white sighs. She waves at something behind us. I glance over my shoulder and spot a security camera mounted high on the wall.

From the outside, the mansion looked to be only three stories, but on the ground floor we step into an iron birdcage elevator and seem to be inside it for a long time, climbing and climbing.

Eventually the elevator doors open and we move into a long rectangular room. We are high above the earth. To my amazement, the Atlantic Ocean is aqua and rollicking. The room is not like the other rooms in the famous author's house. It is not baroque. It looks more like a command center, with white lacquer desks and black rolling chairs, wide computer screens and ringing phones. More women in white pant-suits and black headsets sit in front of the computers, typing furiously. I know at once that these must be the assistants. The relentless activity, the churning industry. The woman in white who brought us up here rings a hanging bell. All the other women stop typing, look up. "They've come to meet the author," the woman in white says.

One strange thing about the command center is that certain details seem to have sprung directly from my imagination—or, more specifically, from my dreams. For one thing, the room is crowded with cats. Tabby cats, white cats, black cats, short-hairs, Scottish folds, Siamese. They saunter across the desks. They unsort paperwork. They nuzzle the women in white. They hiss. They lick themselves. They are curled up in corners or under the white desks, sleeping soundly. They press open their small mouths and display sharp glistening teeth. At the front of the room, I remember my dreams about the famous author in the castle garret, taking dictation from cats. The only difference is that we are now in the garret of a mansion in Palm Beach and I can find no evidence that the cats are offering dictation. Also, there is still no famous author to be found.

A woman stands up from a desk. She is dressed like all the others, in a white pantsuit, but she is the only one with a red carnation tucked inside her jacket lapel. She has dark, straight hair, a long neck, delicate wrists. She starts walking toward us. The other women return to typing. The first woman in white, our guide, moves out into the room, takes a seat at a desk, and begins writing in longhand on a legal pad. The woman with the red carnation leads us over to a conference area by the window, three white leather Art Deco armchairs with a small glass table between them. We sit down. This new woman in white pushes the carnation stem deeper into her lapel. She looks out at the rolling waves. "I understand you're here to meet the author," she says. My sister and I nod. The woman in white steeples her hands. "I am the author." She gestures out into the room, where the other women in white are vigorously working. "Or, rather, we all are."

"The author is dead," the woman in white continues. "More or less." She has smooth brown skin. She's wearing berry lipstick. Her eyelashes are stiff with mascara. "He's been dead for over a decade. ALS, I'm afraid. Such a nasty illness. In the end, you suffocate." Per the author's will, he was cryogenically frozen and is being kept in the catacombs beneath the mansion. Until he can be revived, he wanted his enterprise to continue uninterrupted. And for his collection of carnivorous plants to be kept alive. So the assistants at the time took over, coming up with ideas and writing the books themselves and then—as his popularity grew—hiring ghosts to help. They are responsible for moving his oeuvre away from his more enigmatic early style into a thing the masses crave. The author was—helpfully—a recluse when he was alive. Now, when he must make the occasional public appearance, there is a look-alike actor on retainer. The woman explains that she is technically in charge—she has known the author the longest—but they decided some time ago to dispense with a hierarchical structure and to operate as a collective, taking turns discharging the various duties. I don't mention that being one of their ghosts never felt like joining a collective movement. More like hurling your best attempts at the feet of an implacable parent. "What the fuck *is* this place," my sister says again. The woman in white points a manicured finger at the floor. "Before his death, the author hired scientists to build a cryo-preservation chamber in the mansion's catacombs. So he is always with us, suspended in a bath of liquid nitrogen. Sometimes I take my morning coffee down there. You would not believe the quiet." She rests a hand under her chin and sighs. "In any event, I didn't write that book you came here to ask about. But I was around when it was written."

A black cat bounds into the woman in white's lap, arches its glossy back, and purrs. "The author and the founder of ELECTRA were childhood friends," the woman in white begins. They grew up in the same neighborhood, she tells us. They went to the same private schools. The childhood friend lost their parents at thirteen, in a sailing accident. The parents were grotesquely wealthy, and so this friend inherited a sum of untold proportions. After the tragedy, the friend became a bit of a doomsday prepper. In time, the two of them realized the greatest luxury, the most powerful defense against disaster, was the freedom to leave. Imagine: no matter where you are the emergency evacuation pod is always ready, waiting to ferry you to the next place. *Go where you need to be.* Sure, the friend could have invested in colonizing outer space, but who wants to live on a space station? Mars is a frozen tundra, riddled with volcanoes and desert dust. Wouldn't it be better to travel to a version of the world you already knew? What if the ability to move from one world to another was a product that could be bought and sold? Questions such as these led the author's childhood friend to found ELECTRA. "Now close your eyes and imagine this founder," the woman in white instructs us. "You're probably picturing a man, right? Or at least someone white?" She pauses and looks carefully at us, her eyes widening. "Probably you're not imagining someone like me inhering a sum of untold proportions and coming up with all these ideas. Well, you would be wrong. Most people are. That book you brought with you? For many years, the author was the only person who believed in ELECTRA. Consider *Season of Death* an homage." The woman in white runs her fingernails down the cat's midnight spine. "Of course, we've been following this little MIND'S EYE experiment with great interest. One day, when the technology is refined, it is going to cost a great deal of money to travel from one world to the next. In the meantime, with all these missing people—

well, it's clear there are still some kinks to work out. For one thing, the transitional zones are filled with these little pits, and sometimes people just fall right into them." I lean forward in my chair. I feel a light pulsing at my temples. My armpits are damp. "In my world, I'm just a ghost. What am I to you here?" The woman in white tells me that, in this world, I am an author. "Not a *famous* author," she clarifies. "But still you manage to publish your little books. Art-house feminist eco-thrillers, far too esoteric for the masses. We've offered you many invitations to ghost, all of which you've declined. Despite being such a talented ghost, in your world. Maybe one day you'll wake up and decide to make some real money." The black cat leaps down and claws at my sister's shoelaces. "I have access to the whole chessboard," the woman in white goes on. "At this stage, there are only two versions of reality to travel between, and they are more alike than not." I listen to the click-clack of all the assistants typing. Emailing the other ghosts. Whipping up one story after the next. I ask the woman in white if it bothers her to peddle books that have nothing real or true to say about the world. "Please," she says, with a flick of the hand. "Real and true are overrated, in this line of work. Haven't you seen what it's like out there? Real and true are what people read to get away from."

The woman in white picks up a black remote and presses a button. The Atlantic Ocean dissolves and is replaced with a body of water that looks monstrous: swollen and churning and blue-black. I watch the water darken and pulse. I watch massive waves thrash the shore. The first ocean must have been some kind of hologram screen. The woman in white presses the remote again and the normal-seeming Atlantic is restored. Low, uniform whitecaps cast glistening nets across the sand. "It looks so real," my sister whispers. "We only know what we perceive," the woman in white replies. "And we perceive so very little."

The woman in white ushers us back into the birdcage elevator. Just before we step inside, I feel something soft brush against my ankles and look down. A tabby cat with gold eyes purrs between my legs. My pants are covered in cat hair, and yet the woman in white's pants are spotless. In the elevator, she presses a button and the carriage plummets. The lights flicker and dim; my ears pop. In the catacombs, the ceiling is low and dewed with water. I smell sulfur. We follow the woman in white down a narrow stone tunnel. My sister grips my arm, her nails biting into my skin. Motion sensor lights flash. The woman in white turns left and then right; I feel like we're being led through a maze. Finally we arrive at a heavy steel door. We pass through the door and she switches on a light. We're standing in front of a rectangular window, looking into a small room. A silver carapace sits in the center, surrounded by a mist. It looks like something that has been recovered from outer space. "Well, there he is," the woman in white says. "That's a cryonic vessel, packed with liquid nitrogen and frozen to −196 degrees Celsius. All his organs have been perfectly preserved, of course. Still, this is a far cry from what he was like when he was alive. A little eccentric, but also great fun. He loved musicals, practical jokes." She presses an intercom button. "Well," she says. "You've come all this way. Go on. Don't let a little cryonic vessel intimidate you. What would you like to tell him?"

I cannot think of a single appropriate thing to say to a cryogenically frozen person. A person who, until very recently, I believed to be my employer. The person I was writing toward. I step a little closer to the intercom. The room is freezing cold. I clear my throat and then press the button. "Everything is *not* as it seems," I say to the famous author. "You were certainly right about that."

The woman in white tells us that the famous author did not believe that death was as clear-cut as most people think. For example, he has been dead for years and yet, in the minds of millions, he is very much alive. "Although I suppose to be cryogenically frozen is to be suspended in a liminal state. At least if you believe in that sort of thing. Me? It was never my place to tell him how to live or how to die, but one thing I can say for sure is that if he ever wakes up I think he's going to be pretty disappointed by what he finds."

On the way back to the elevators, I notice a light flashing at the other end of the stone tunnel. "What's that?" I ask the woman in white. She claps once and trots over to another steel door, moving with a fresh buoyancy, her kitten heels clicking across the floor. This door has a round window in the center. I cup my hands around my eyes and peer through the glass. I find another command center—computer screens, headsets—only it's an inversion of the one upstairs. All the women are dressed in black pantsuits. The long desks are black lacquer and the chairs are white. My sister nudges me out of the way to look. "You want to talk about storytelling?" the woman in white says. "You want to talk about real and true?" Her cheeks flush. She speaks with the unbridled pride of a new parent. The light from the window spotlights the carnation in her lapel; the flower glows like a small ruby. "These ELECTRA coders are the *real* storytellers. They are writing stories we can actually live inside. As much as we try and keep the plots au courant, the novel is, I'm afraid, a pretty outdated technology."

I look through the window again. Something caught my eye the first time and I can still feel its presence in my field of vision, like an eyelash or a grain of sand. It's the two women, the two identical women, seated at a long desk. They're facing the door, their fingers moving furiously across keyboards. For a moment, their pale hands lift. They look at each other. Their mouths open and shut. All the while their long fingers keep tapping at air. "Can we go inside?" I ask the woman in white. She tells us that the coders are hard at work building virtual worlds—different worlds, better worlds—and cannot, under any circumstances, be disturbed.

"Did you see—" I start to ask my sister. I keep my voice low. In the tunnel, the woman in white walks briskly ahead. My sister grabs my hand and nods. "How do we get in?" She squeezes my fingers so tightly I think the bones might break. "I'm thinking," she says. "I'm thinking as hard as I can."

The woman in white steps inside the birdcage elevator. The doors slide shut behind her, locking her in and us out. She whirls around and stabs at the buttons, but the doors do not open. An alarm sounds. Red lights flash along the sides of the ceiling. She wraps her fingers around the ornate metal, tries to shake the cage. "What is the meaning of this?" she cries out. "We pulled the fire alarm," two voices say from behind. "So she's not going anywhere for a minute." My sister and I spin around. The twins are standing there, in their black pantsuits. They're each carrying a small black backpack.

The woman in white slams her palms against the metal. "Just what are you doing?" we ask the twins. "We know who you are," they say. "We've been trying to find you for months."

We run down the stone tunnel. I feel chased by the flashing lights. We hit a dead end. The twins pull a black lever in the wall and a trapdoor opens. We crawl down a steel ladder and into a network of underground tunnels. "The famous author was obsessed with Walt Disney," the twins tell us. "He wanted an elaborate subterranean system underneath the mansion, like they have at EPCOT." Eventually we climb up another ladder and emerge through a manhole, into the daylight. I scramble to my feet and see that we're just outside the mansion. I lean down and pull my sister out of the hole. We race across the driveway and into the car. We speed right through the boom barrier and into rush hour traffic.

The twins start talking and don't stop for a long time. My sister pulls over into a parking lot the size of a football field. Her hands strangle the steering wheel. Her golden eyes darken. Blood drips from her nostrils. "I can't believe it," she keeps saying. "I can't believe this is happening. I thought I was on a mission. I thought I was communicating with Dad in the afterlife. I thought he chose *me*." In my notebook, I attempt to describe the exact color of the blood oozing down my sister's face. *Carmine, crimson, oxblood.*

. . .

It was never our father in MIND'S EYE. His presence in the English garden was a manipulation, like the woman in white's fake Atlantic Ocean.

During the lockdown, the twins explain, ELECTRA embedded portals into MIND'S EYE. This was intended to be a road test, to gauge the side effects of traveling to other worlds. The unforeseen complications. All those people trapped in their homes with nothing better to do than use their devices. ELECTRA knew the experiment would yield a robust sample size. Around the same time, the twins' father started appearing in their dreams. *I want you to do something.* The twins, who are expert coders, began trying to reach us through my sister's device. "We didn't think it was working, our attempts to lure you over here," they tell us. "But then today we look up and you're right there, on the security cameras at the mansion." My sister wipes her nose on her T-shirt, leaves the fabric streaked with blood. "Why didn't you just use the portals yourselves and find us in our world?" she asks, her voice quivering. "Why did you have to trick me?" The twins look at each other. They pinch the little black buttons on their silk blouses. "The technology is still nascent," they reply. "There's a reason why all those headsets were distributed to people who belong to another world. We have our problems over here, but it's nothing like where you've come from."

. . .

"Will you stop writing everything down?" My sister leans over and flips my notebook shut. "I can't concentrate when I feel like every little thing I say is being recorded." She leans back in her seat and presses her fingertips into her eyeballs. "Are you, like, a journalist?" the twins ask me. "Because we signed NDAs." I shake my head, slide my notebook and pen back into my purse.

We ask the twins when and how their father died, in this world, and they tell us he's not technically dead yet.

Their father, our father, is in a coma. He fell ill during the pandemic and he has been in a coma for months. He is not alive, in the fullest sense of the word, but also he is not dead. My sister and I beg the twins to take us to the hospital. At Florida Mercy, we find the same punishing lights and blade-sharp corners that we remember from our world. We spill into his hospital room first, the twins hovering behind us. I hear the terrible burble of machines. "I can't do this again." My sister lurches into me. "I made a mistake." The man in the hospital bed is identical to our father. I take my sister's hand. We creep closer. His lips are pale and dry. His skin looks waxed. "Dad," we say. "Is that you?" It occurs to me now that my sister and I have undertaken a pilgrimage, and

this was always our destination. Like Lazarus, our father has
been resurrected. I feel a clawing longing for my husband,
who knows all about the ways of pilgrims and might understand what it is we're supposed to do next. The twins tell
us that they were a little surprised when their father started
appearing in their dreams. They were the product of an affair
and he was an occasional parent, at best. The odd birthday or
weekend trip to the Keys. "And then all of a sudden he was in
this coma and then in our dreams, giving orders," the twins
say. "He was very convincing. Still, we weren't sure if we were
being conned. Like when he used to 'borrow' our allowance
on weekend trips and refuse to pay us back. He never would
explain *why* we needed to find you two."

On the rolling tray table next to his bed, I find a plastic cup
of orange juice, the foil half torn away. A quarter (tails). Red
drugstore reading glasses with a hairline crack in one of the
lenses. Artifacts from a life.

One of the twins sticks her head out into the hall. "Other-
you is coming," she says, pointing a finger at me. "She's coming down the hallway right now." They tell us that this half
sister won't even acknowledge their existence and that her
books are filled with toxic half siblings who are always out to
ruin lives with their twisted plans. She is a hostile presence,

in other words. We hustle out of the room and into a bath-room. We each lock ourselves in a stall, where we will wait until the coast is clear. Seconds later, a door swings open. A pair of black patent flats appears. I stand on the toilet and peer over the top of the stall. A familiar-looking woman stares into the mirror. She whispers something to herself. She looks the way I imagine I might have if I had finished my PhD and become a scholar instead of a ghost. She's wear-ing jeans, a white blouse, a blazer, tortoiseshell glasses. Her hair is cut to her chin. She's holding a slim paperback in one hand, with her name—our name, which has never appeared on any of the books I have actually written—splashed across the front.

When she leaves the bathroom, I creep out behind her. She enters our father's room. She leaves the door ajar. I hover outside the doorway. I watch her pull a chair to his bedside and hold up the paperback. "Hot off the presses," she says. She opens the book and begins to read.

She might look like me, but she doesn't sound like me. She has a crisp, practiced reading voice. Even from the hallway I can make out every word. The story is set at some point in the future, when humans have, due to an unnamed mass trauma, lost the ability to speak. They can only communicate through AI, which reads their thoughts and translates them into text. But the AI is always mistranslating and misunderstanding, which causes countless problems. The protagonist is a linguist, and she discovers that the AI is messing up on purpose—but why? And to what end? In one scene, the linguist wants to say something so badly that she beats her fists against her head until she loses consciousness.

I feel a presence behind me and I know it's my sister. The smell of her, the unfathomable intimacy of having known someone their entire life. I was in the room when she came out of our mother, shriveled and red and squalling. She wraps her long arms around my waist. I grab onto her strong wrists. For a moment, we listen together like this, holding fast to each other as the hospital churns around us. From the hallway, I can see a sliver of our father in bed. I watch for movement, but he is perfectly still under the thin white sheets. Nevertheless, he is the reason we are here. "The dad I know would have hated this story," my sister whispers. It's true that our father was never one for outlandish make-believe. Except when it came to his own life.

In the hospital parking lot, we pile back into the car. The twins slide off their black jackets, cuff their silk shirtsleeves. Their pants still appear freshly ironed, one neat crease down each leg. They look like glamorous undertakers. "Your turn," the twins say. "You died during the pandemic," my sister begins. She tells the twins that they will die here in six months' time, when their neighborhood floods. That is why their father wanted them to find us. "You think your world is so much better than ours?" my sister says. "Just you wait." The twins might have been responsible for putting our father in my sister's English garden, but once there he seems to have acquired an independent intelligence, transformed into a presence with his own agenda. "Why wouldn't he have warned us?" the twins want to know. "Maybe," I offer, "he thought it would be too much for you to take in all at once, that you're dead in one world and doomed in the other and your half sisters from a different reality have been put on a mission to save you." That the safest thing for them to do now is to come back with us to our world, to become a kind of ghost. We ask the twins what it is they want to do.

At the Pompano Beach exit, I think the large animal trotting down the emergency lane is just an overfed dog. Upon closer inspection, however, I realize the animal is not a dog but a wolf. As the wolf passes, our fellow travelers press their faces to their windows. They honk and catcall. They record videos on their phones. "Is that a coyote?" the twins ask, straining against their seat belts. I shake my head. I tell her that wolves are bigger than coyotes, with longer tails. Wolves have broader faces and darker noses. They have short round ears, whereas a coyote's are tall and pointy. "How do you know

so much about wolves?" the twins want to know, and I tell
them that I lived with a wolf as a child. We watch the wolf
continue down the emergency lane. The animal does not acknowledge the leering motorists, like a celebrity who cannot
be bothered. "I'm sorry," the twins reply. "Did you just say
that you lived *with* a *wolf* as a *child*?" I explain that it was a
temporary situation and everyone emerged unscathed, except perhaps the wolf. A black van speeds up alongside the
wolf and swerves in front of its path. Men in tactical gear
flood out. The animal attempts to run but is captured with a
large net.

We drive back to the Giant Orange. The twins unzip their
black backpacks and pull out white MIND'S EYE headsets. My sister switches off the ignition and reclines her seat.
I imagine us all awakening to our own virtual world, one
that is private but also interconnected. I imagine us all en-
countering the glistening sunlight, the beautiful and terrifying soundlessness, the saturated colors—and wondering if
we should stay nestled in this virtual cradle, where there is
no weather or noise or catastrophe, for as long as we can. I
remember what the woman in white said about the pits in
the transitional zones. How will we know if we are close to
one? I imagine the sticky darkness that infiltrated my sister's house during the Major Weather Event. A black hole's
gravitational throb. An avalanche of static, shadow.

. . .

When I remove my headset, the Giant Orange is tilted in the earth, as if a sinkhole might be threatening. The sky is streaked with pink and orange. My sister takes off her MIND'S EYE and shakes her head. The twins are still in the back seat, looking a little dazed, with their white headsets around their pale necks. I text my husband our ETA. *We've been worried sick*, he replies. *You've been gone for three days!* As we pull into town, we pass a group of people clustered together on a street corner, holding out signs advocating for the voluntary human extinction movement. HONK IF YOU THINK PEOPLE ARE THE PROBLEM. From what I can observe, Jesus fared much better.

BECOME WHO
YOU ARE

JULY 15–X

Ghosts

When I came back from the Institute, I announced to my family that I wanted to be a writer. No one had any idea what I was talking about. *Write what?* my mother kept asking me. She believed that we should aspire to do something useful with our lives. To be of service. *Write stories*, I kept answering back. I was very excited to actually want to do something besides drink myself into unconsciousness. My father was the only one who tried to understand. Maybe it was because he thought writers were lawless, in their way. Once, I showed him an early attempt at writing a story and he said, *This is some weird shit, but I think you should keep going.* I didn't listen. By then I found my father's overall judgment so suspect I was leery of taking his advice on anything. So I decided that maybe it would be better to study literature instead, which was how I ended up in the doctoral program, and then I thought maybe it would be better to use my own words to write someone else's stories, which was how I became a ghost. The truth is I was scared. Scared that my mother was right and that stories were largely useless. Scared that my father was right and that the only thing for me to do was to keep going. My father never approved of my becoming a student of literature or a ghost. "A waste of your talent," he said about both.

· · ·

The twins have now commandeered the attic room, so I write in bed, like Truman Capote. One thing a lot of people don't know about Capote is that the killers he became obsessed with, the killers who made him famous, are believed by some to have committed a similar murder (a couple and two children, shot and beaten) near Sarasota. The work is slow and uncertain, and at times I'm not sure if what I'm writing down counts as fact or fiction. I am attempting to document the world as accurately as I can, even if that means I have to make things up. I try to forget everything I learned from being a ghost. There are no more emails from the assistants. No more outlines to fill in. I do not consult the internet. I go looking for a new form.

I start writing down one detail a day. The tangerine sunsets. The musk of my dog's paw. The empty wine bottle I find in the bushes (strawberry moscato). I write about the split second, in the transitional zone, when I felt shadows rushing alongside me and I nearly turned in their direction, hurled myself in. I write about the man I hear crying out in the concrete block of a public restroom down by the lake, his anguish amplified by the thick walls. I record the details of a recent holdup at the EZ Pawn (the stolen items include a power saw, tennis racquets, several collectible baseballs, various knives). I write about the house a few blocks over that always seems to have a different kind of pet in the backyard: a rooster, a yappy white Chihuahua, a giant tortoise that creeps with glacial slowness across the lawn. The woman I spotted late one night in an illuminated garage, surrounded by cars on metal lifts. She was in a denim dress, barefoot, dancing alone to salsa. The man in American flag pants pushing a grocery cart filled with empty bottles along the side of the interstate on a blistering day. One leg for stripes, one for stars. I write about Mr. Heaven's hot, succulent bags of boiled peanuts. I write about the knife I find sticking out of an anthill. I write about states of suffering and states of paradise and try to understand how a person can travel from one to the other. With these fragments I slowly begin to build a world. I go where I need to be. I write about the time my former best friend and I kissed each other through a sheet. Memory is a place too, after all. I write about how I sometimes write notes to my father on lined cards and then stick them in a drawer. I want whoever reads this to understand that we believe in a clear line between "living" and "dead," but at the same time we believe that the living can speak to the dead and that the dead can hear us and even, on occasion, speak back.

I do not tell anyone that I am writing these things down. Not even my husband. Not even my dog. I imagine people from another planet, from another dimension in space and time, discovering this document many years in the future. I imagine them using it to understand what happened.

. . .

Writing a story cannot bring back the dead, but it can draw them a little closer to the world of the living. The moment I start writing about my father he begins appearing in my dreams. He does not ask me for anything. He does not dispense orders. He just observes me from a distance, a bystander, and always I walk toward him, try to bridge the distance between us, but it is not a gap that can be closed.

After these dreams, I ponder that other version of myself I saw in the hospital, who can sit at her father's bedside and read to him and yet at the same time remain separated by a ceaseless silence.

I ponder the version of myself that was lost to the wilderness, that slid into a pit and never came out. I don't need to travel to other realities to confront this other self, however. She is with me every day of my life.

I decide to believe that these dreams about my father are a sign that I'm on the right track.

To write is to attempt to bridge the gaps that cannot ever be closed.

In the next Ask Ava column, the letter writer is seeking advice for a situation concerning her aunt. Shortly after the Major Weather Event, her aunt started spending a lot of time at another house in the neighborhood. At first, the house seemed like a gathering place for people who wanted to share their pains and experiences, to undertake a few good works in the community, but then her aunt moved into the house and started wearing a gray sweatsuit and standing on street corners with a sign that read SAVE THE EARTH DON'T GIVE BIRTH. One morning, the letter writer went over to the house where her aunt has been spending so much time and discovered a dozen or so people milling around in the front yard, all in the same gray sweatsuits. Now she is worried that her aunt has joined a cult. *Cults are very seductive*, Ava says, *because they are portals to another world.* Ava suggests the letter writer lure her aunt away from the site of the cult—which I recognize as my mother's house—with her favorite food and then trap her in a vehicle and drive her around to all the places that are integral to her identity until she remembers who she is, where she comes from, where she really wants to be going.

• • •

One afternoon I ask Arizona where she got all the gray sweatsuits from, and she admits that she bought them in bulk at Walmart.

Florida has attracted a number of cult leaders through the years, like Cyrus Teed, who fled Chicago and an ocean of debt for the steaming wilderness of Estero. In 1894, Teed founded a utopian commune called the Koreshan Unity. The Koreshans believed that we lived on a concave earth, that our human universe existed underneath the firm shell of the globe. They believed that inside the hollow sphere there was boundless life and that outside lay a nothingness, a terrible void. The Koreshans believed in reincarnation and in collectivism. They believed that the sun was an invisible electromagnetic battery. That what we thought was the sun was merely a reflection—the moon and the stars were reflections too. They believed that celibacy was the secret to immortality, a theory that was debunked by Teed's own death, which was far from utopian. He was badly beaten after a group of Koreshans got into a fight with a group of non-Koreshans outside a grocery store in Fort Myers. His followers kept vigil over his dead body and awaited resurrection. They thought he would rise like a saint. Instead Teed's body decayed to such an extent that a county health officer intervened, ordering that Teed be buried. In 1921, a hurricane struck Estero Island and dragged Teed's coffin out into the sea.

. . .

In the end, my sisters and I tell everyone a modified version of the truth: the ELECTRA headsets were designed to brainwash their users, to turn people deranged, and some of these deranged people went missing as a result. "But why would ELECTRA want to make people deranged?" my husband prods us one morning. "In order to have power over them," the twins reply. To my surprise, he seems satisfied by this response. "Power," he repeats, stirring his coffee with a butter knife. Power explains everything.

For a time, my mother and her followers change their signs to warn people away from the headsets. HONK IF YOU WANT TO BE IN THE REAL WORLD. Arizona leads a door-knocking campaign and rounds up nearly all the headsets in the neighborhood. My mother writes a post on Nextdoor: *Attention, neighbors! There is a defect in your MIND'S EYE. Destroy them at once.* We hope that word will spread.

The twins—how can I even begin to describe them? They believe that they can communicate with each other telepathically. They know how to code. They love to cook and have a deep repertoire of vegetarian stews—chickpea, lentil, Tuscan bean. The house turns fragrant with garlic, za'atar. My mother is warm to the twins, as they are irrefutable evidence of the many accusations she has, through the years, leveled against my father. "Good morning, girls," she says when they come downstairs. She always brews extra coffee for them, even though they prefer matcha. At lunchtime, she eats their soups with gusto. She even tolerates their skepticism about the voluntary human extinction movement. "Isn't the real problem the allocation of resources?" the twins say at a meeting. "For example, the birth rate in the United States has been falling for years and yet our greenhouse gas emissions continue to rise." My mother points out that without people there would be no resources to allocate. "This movement is about attacking the problem at the root," she insists. "But think of how long that will take," the twins counter. "For the root to wither and die. What makes you think we have that kind of time?" They have refused Arizona's gray sweatsuits. One afternoon, they went out to investigate an estate sale and returned with clothes that looked like they came from a tennis camp, white terry-cloth shorts and pink polo shirts. I will think to myself that I am absolutely nothing like these stone-cold weirdos, but then a second later I'll catch it: the way they hold a fork or laugh at a joke with their heads tipped back and one hand held up like they mean to put a stop to something. They know how to read tarot. Every day they draw three cards. The first represents the past, the second the present, the third the future. The twins never tell us what the future cards reveal. Sometimes they look at the card for a very long time and from different angles, as if they can't quite believe what they're seeing. Sometimes they just turn the future card over and start to cry.

· · ·

My sister and I FaceTime our half brother, so he can meet the twins. They spend the entire morning blow-drying their hair into soft auburn waves and applying thick layers of makeup. They starch the collars of their pink polos. They insist on taking the call from the living room sofa, to get the best light. When my half brother sees the faces of his half sisters, he raises a hand, his fingers stretching forward, as though it might be possible to reach through the screen and touch them. All five of us, I realize, have our father's hands. The long fingers, the oval nail beds. The filaments of the DNA that binds us. "Who are all those people?" my half brother says when he notices the gray suits wandering around behind us. Before the call, my mother's followers presented my dog with a crown of dried flowers and tiny animal bones. "And why are they all dressed the same?" I explain that my mother has—perhaps unwittingly—become a cult leader, though the nature of her cult is relatively benign. My half brother reports that a sinkhole recently opened on his street, so massive that the residents cannot leave the neighborhood. Most people are afraid to even step outside. He tells us that a neighbor dropped a coconut into the sinkhole, just to see what would happen. It fell so far that no one heard a sound—a thud, a crack—when it eventually hit the ground. For all they know that coconut could still be falling.

A wolf makes our local news. The animal escaped from the compound of a former dictator turned real estate mogul in

Miami. The dictator turned mogul sent a recovery team out in pursuit of the wolf. They have dropped nets and fired tranquilizer darts, but this wolf has evaded every attempt at capture. The twins shudder when they see the wolf lope across our TV screen. They are fearful of dogs; apparently they were both bitten as children, when their father took them on a weekend outing to the Flagler Dog Track. "I hope someone catches that creature soon," they say. "I hope it doesn't just keep running wild." Such an outcome is seeming less and less likely considering that the wolf was last spotted entering the Apalachicola National Forest.

One morning I find that my belly button has sealed itself back up. Now the center of my stomach is smooth, with a pink blotch where the little tunnel used to be. The area has a sheen to it, like a fresh burn. In a few days the blotch fades and there is no evidence that I ever had a belly button at all. "Do you think this is a fatal condition?" I ask my husband. I wonder if this physical transformation has anything to do with the pilgrimage I made to that other world. He bends down. "Probably not." In our bedroom, he strokes my smooth stomach. "I mean, what are belly buttons even for?" He starts listing the creatures that do not have belly buttons. Snakes, lizards, fish. He stares at me in wonder. He takes my hand and squeezes. I can tell we're both thinking the same thing. Am I changing—slowly, perhaps too slowly, or maybe just slowly enough—into something that can survive underwater?

Trauma can alter us in the most unexpected ways.

A trauma leaves behind a pit, it's true, but there's always the chance something worthy will rise up from the muck.

Why are my husband and I still here? Sometimes, late at night, we talk dreamily about leaving my mother's house and going back to the little city in upstate New York where we used to live. On nights like this, I lie with my head on his firm chest. The dog paddles his legs in his dreams. We reminisce about the symphony hall and the wine bar and the absence of the Confederate flag. But who are we kidding? We can't leave the people we love to go under with the ship. We have to keep helping them bail out water. Also, who is to say that the place we left, the place that we remember together in bed, still exists as it once did? To return might well be a journey that we can now only undertake in our imaginations.

Since the beginning, people have told stories in order to save themselves, but there are certain things that stories cannot save us from.

In Florida, the reports of missing persons dwindle. We hold our breath. We wait to see what will happen next.

A lot happens next and none of it is good. The first time my niece sees water gushing through the storm drains and the grates, she points at the churning froth and says, "Hose?" The sky is a flat sheet of blue; in fact, I have not seen a cloud in many days, cumulus or otherwise. The water is coming from someplace deep underground. A wound in the earth that we cannot see.

In the next Ask Ava column, the letter writer is the same man who wrote in some weeks ago, to seek advice about his missing mother. He tells Ava that his mother has returned without any explanation. He was driving to work when he spotted her in a nearby park, in her regular clothes, clutching her MIND'S EYE to her chest like a life raft. She was not able to say where she'd been or what had happened, but when he pried away her headset she did not, for once, object. She is the same person, his mother, but also she is different. She rises at dawn and drinks her coffee outside. He will peer through his bedroom window and find her staring hard at the sky. On occasion, he overhears her humming an unfamiliar song. What happened to her? At the end of the letter, he admits that he did not dispose of her MIND'S EYE. He keeps the white headset on his bedside table. He knows he should just get rid of the thing, but he can't bring himself to do it. His mother is changed, even if he can't quite put his finger on how. Perhaps she went where she needed to. He has started longing to go where he needs to be, even if he can't say where exactly that is. Is it so wrong, he asks, to want to find out?

The cats return to the neighborhood. One morning, I'm walking the dog and I see cats everywhere: they are huddled together on front porches; they are nestled in the boughs of trees; they are crouched in the parks. We walk past a trio of black cats perched on the back of a bench, purring loudly at one another. The longer I watch the cats, the more I get the sense that they are moving as one body, that the cats lounging on the sun-dappled front porches are somehow communicating with the cats in the trees. My dog is cowed by the presence of all these cats. He walks with timid, soft steps, head low, eyes wide. We pass a calico cat sitting on a fire hydrant that has been colonized by a green vine with yellow flowers. This vine doesn't normally bloom so late in the year and yet the cat sits atop a throne of golden blossoms. Catclaw.

In 1961, one hundred members of wealthy families banded together to construct a private bomb shelter in Mount Dora. This subterranean fortress is roughly the size of a motel, built six feet under an orange grove. Thousands of square feet of underground living space, stocked with enough food and fuel to allow one hundred people to exist for months. The founders anticipated emerging into a nuclear wasteland, where they would then rebuild society from the ground up. They claimed to have been inspired by the novel *Alas, Babylon*, about a nuclear strike on a small Florida town. The bomb shelter was—is—the largest privately owned shelter in the nation. In 1971, the families sold the shelter to a single buyer, who wished to remain anonymous. All that is known to the public is that the entrance is located in a backyard shed, and, after his young son climbed down into the fortress and temporarily went missing, the man had the shelter sealed shut. By now that man is dead and his son is the owner of the property. The son has unsealed the bomb shelter and is accepting applications for up to twenty-five residents, per an ad placed in the local newspaper.

. . .

A militia captures the Kennedy Space Center, for the purpose of commandeering the launchpad and the rockets, though it remains to be seen what they intend to use them for. In Homestead, another militia takes over the Coral Castle, built by an eccentric who single-handedly carved over a thousand tons of coral rock between 1923 and 1951. His coral kingdom includes towers, walls, a telescope, a nine-ton gate, and a "Repentance Center," where a person can wedge their head into a hole cut from the rock and meditate on where they went wrong.

Florida is the envy of America, our Cro-Magnon governor says at a public address. *Florida is a beacon. There is no reason to be afraid. This is what it feels like to break free from tyranny. Soon our way of life will spread across the entire country.* He pauses to survey the crowd. His thick forehead shimmers with sweat. *You ain't seen nothing yet.*

My father-in-law reports that the whole country is watching Florida now. In New Jersey, the news anchors are talking about Florida like it is a test case. The first point on the map that appears to be in the early stages of some kind of dissolution. Whether it is temporary or permanent remains to be seen. Officials from other states are warning their citizens against traveling to Florida, as though this land is harboring something contagious. Some people are defying these orders, however. They are making pilgrimages to Florida. They listened to our Cro-Magnon governor's address and somehow they heard the word "utopia."

I'm out in the yard with the gray suits, shoveling fresh soil into raised beds. "Psst," my sister says through the fence. "Are you busy?" I go over to her. I dust the dirt from my hands. "I'm here." She says she has something she needs to tell me. "Go ahead," I say. I listen to her breathe on the other side of the fence. "I'm pregnant," she says.

This second baby gives my sister the worst morning sickness of her life. She vomits day and night, into the toilet for the most part, but also sometimes into the kitchen sink and in the backyard and on the side of the road. One afternoon, my sister and I lie in her bed together. We hold hands. We stare up at the ceiling. My brother-in-law comes into the room and places a ginger ale on her bedside table, his face a cloud of worry. We have decided to not advertise news of her pregnancy for the time being, given the nature of our mother's cult. They recently had pamphlets printed, with the statistic about disposable diapers taking centuries to decompose right there at the top. I reach over and place my hand on her hot stomach. "I feel like I'm possessed," she moans. "Possessed by a demon that won't fucking quit. What if this thing turns out like Rosemary's Baby?" I roll onto my side and notice that my sister's eyes have been transformed. The golden irises are now a dark and verdant green. Like the color of kelp found in the depths of the ocean.

"Can I show you something?" My sister slides a hand into her pocket, pulls out her phone. She tells me that she took a video of our father in the hospital, on the night he died. "I took it while he was sleeping," she says. The video is forty-seven seconds long. It was recorded after our father tore off his clothes and demanded to be taken home, after he was sedated and returned to bed. She is the only other person in the room. My half brother and I are out there somewhere, racing through the night. The lights are low. I can see her shadow flickering near the foot of the bed. Death is slinking down the hallway, but the terrible hour has not yet arrived. Our father lies long and straight. Palms down. Eyes closed. The dome of his head is covered in a silver fuzz, like a baby bird. I can see the shapes of his large feet through the thin blankets. I rest my head on my sister's warm shoulder. In the background, I can hear her hoarse, trembling voice. She is whispering the words to a song I can remember our father singing to us when we were children.

After she falls asleep, I root around in the kitchen in search of tea. I open a ceramic jar shaped like an alligator and find a pair of red reading glasses with a thin crack in one lens. I pick them up and put them on. The world around me quivers and sways. They are the reading glasses that were on other-dad's bedside table in the hospital room. My sister must have swiped them when no one was looking.

In medieval times, the success of a pilgrimage was gauged in part by the relics a pilgrim brought home. The relics were proof of all the pilgrim had witnessed and endured; they gave physical form to the experiences that were beyond what could be described with language. When Hugh of Lincoln, a twelfth-century bishop, visited a monastery in Normandy, he was shown the arm of Mary Magdalene. Hugh sliced away the covering and tried to break off a sliver of bone. He then raised the arm to his mouth and bit off a finger. The monks, horrified, reported him attacking the arm of Mary Magdalene like a ravenous dog. Later, a whole economy would spring up around relics, with hucksters selling pig bones that they claimed to be the remnants of saints.

Not all relics were physical possessions, however. Saint Fursey claimed, during a pilgrimage, to have received a vision of the afterlife so powerful he was left with scorch marks and a propensity to sweat even in frigid temperatures.

. . .

At night, my husband and I can hear the twins moving around in the attic room. Creak, crack. The twins were gymnasts in high school. I imagine them doing handstands above us, holding those inverted poses for hours, the blood rushing to their faces. Lately they have been trying to teach my niece to cartwheel. The twins are naturals at talking to children. "Do you know the story of Noah?" they ask my niece one afternoon, after she inquires about the water that keeps spraying through sewers and grates, soaking the streets. "Noah and the Flood?" It is a particular kind of insanity to parent children who are still rolling around in that newly verbal stew, the utter horror of having to explain this world (this world!) to a nascent person. By the time my niece can fully grasp what's happening she'll probably wish she could crawl back inside my sister's womb and float forever in an amniotic dream-sea. "I know Noah," my niece says. The twins tell her that when the time comes we'll have to run around the neighborhood and save as many animals as we can.

"Even the dogs?" my niece asks. "Yes," the twins say, grudgingly. "Even the dogs."

"When is the time?" my niece asks next, and the twins tell her the truth: That nobody knows exactly. The time could be near or it could be far. All we know for sure is that every day we get closer.

Late one night, I get an email from the head woman in white, informing me that I have a choice. Option 1: I can move into the Palm Beach mansion, sign an NDA, don a white pantsuit, and join their hive. She points out that the mansion has been designed to weather a number of disaster scenarios: plagues, floods, civil war, insurrection. *It's the least you can do, considering that you took two of my best employees, and besides you're far too talented to remain a ghost.* Option 2: I can quit. I ask the woman in white if the famous author is cryogenically frozen in this version of our world, and she tells me that she cannot confirm or deny any of the differences between the two realities I have experienced. She cannot confirm or deny if there are, in fact, different realities at all.

I quit.

She's right, I think, after I submit my resignation. The novel *is* a pretty outdated technology, but that is exactly why we need it. The form is so archaic that it can't be fucked with.

. . .

That same week, I get an email from the assistant to a pro-secession Florida state representative. The assistant is looking for a ghost, has heard I'm on the market. The state rep wants to write the story of his life—as an autobiography or a political thriller or a manifesto; the form has yet to be determined—but the problem is that he can barely string a sentence together, according to his assistant. She is not even sure he knows all the letters in the alphabet. The most important thing about his future book is that he be portrayed as an American hero, a cowboy, a salt-of-the-earth, wholly non-elite freethinker. Even if he went to Yale and is terrified of horses. The assistant wants to know if I am interested in bringing his vision to life. I reply with a video of a tiger mauling the poacher who killed the tiger's entire family. The tiger tracked the poacher through the wilderness for a week, attacked under the cover of night.

My husband gets a call from his father, who tells him he has started reading Nietzsche. So far he has made it through *On the Genealogy of Morality* and *The Birth of Tragedy* and *The Antichrist*. When my husband asks his father why he has started reading Nietzsche, he says that it just seemed like the right time. "Nietzsche was nuts," he concludes before too long. Nietzsche's family would have agreed: they committed him to an asylum, where he lived for eleven years before dying at the age of fifty-five.

. . .

I know this because Nietzsche was one of the writers my old English teacher told me about, when she came to visit me at the Institute.

Become who you are! In the end, that is the only Nietzsche line that my father-in-law thinks is worth remembering.

How can we tell when we have become who we are? And who does a changed and changing world demand that we become?

In the next Ask Ava column, the letter writer, a woman in her twenties, tells Ava that she didn't shave for several days and then in the shower she noticed that her hair hadn't grown back. Her legs, her underarms, her bikini line—all the hair is still gone. Also, the hair has vanished from her forearms, her upper lip. She's stopped sweating, even when it's hot outside. *And it's always hot outside*, she writes. In bed at night, she feels a strange crackling in her vertebrae. *Have you ever heard ice breaking up?* she asks Ava. *It sounds like that.* Plus every time she pulls back her lips in the mirror her teeth look a little smaller. *I know I should be consulting a doctor and not an advice columnist*, she writes. *But I'm scared. Our world feels so unstable. Do you think all this could be caused by stress?* By way of reply Ava recounts the Greek myth of Deucalion and Pyrrha, who wandered a flooded earth until they arrived at the mountaintop of Parnassus. The goddess Themis instructed the couple to throw stones behind them as they walked. The stones thrown by Deucalion turned into men, the ones by Pyrrha turned into women, and, in this way, humanity was given another chance.

At the voluntary human extinction meetings, I overhear whisperings about the curious physical symptoms people are experiencing. Lost eyelashes, oddly dry armpits, fingernails that soften and fall away like petals. None of these symptoms are painful—just very strange. From what I can ascertain, the only thing the afflicted have in common is that they got sick during the pandemic. *The worst fever of my life*, one gray suit tells me. She's wearing floral gardening gloves to hide her disintegrating fingernails. *I felt like I was being cooked.*

That night, in my notebook, I add a storyline about a pandemic that has altered the survivors in ways they have not yet even dared to imagine.

My husband is out all day, and when he returns he tells me about the journey he has been on. That morning, he was running along the lake when he bumped into the bike man, who was still missing his dog. There were other shelters he could check, but they were far away and someone had slashed the front tire of his bike. My husband offered to give the bike man a ride, said they could check the shelters together. In the car, the bike man told him the story of how he and the white dog found each other in the first place. He has been sober for years, but he used to drink. One night, he passed out in a park. He was so loaded that he'd forgotten his own name and his mother's name and the name of his hometown. He said that he drank to forget, but when the forgetting actually happened he was terrified. He shut his eyes and drifted away on this sea of forgetting, not expecting to wake, and when he did a white dog was standing over him, licking his face. *I thought I was dead*, the bike man said, *and that the dog was an angel welcoming me into heaven. And I was a little surprised because I have done some things that God might frown upon. Then I realized that I was alive, that all this was happening right here on earth, but I still think that dog is an angel.* After hours of searching, they found the dog at an overflow shelter in Kissimmee. When the handlers opened the cage, the white dog leaped into the bike man's arms and they spun around in that desolate concrete hall like old dance partners. He carried the dog away from the shelter and into my husband's car, where the dog bit a hunk out of the back seat. "It looks like I had a shark riding around in there," my husband tells me. The bike man found a classical music station on the radio, because the dog likes Mozart. And it was true. When the *Requiem* came on the dog sat upright in the back seat like a person and gazed out the window, as though Mozart was triggering a distant yet powerful memory.

The manatees start appearing in the springs, which is not what is supposed to happen. Normally they only come in the winter. Something in the water is changing. I take my niece to see them and explain that, believe it or not, the manatee is a close relation of the elephant.

In 1493, Christopher fucking Columbus mistook three manatees for mermaids and was gravely disappointed that they were not as beautiful as he had been led to believe mermaids were from maritime paintings.

On the way home from the springs, my niece tells me that her pet ghost has been sad lately. "He keeps trying to eat the dirt in the backyard," she says, scrunching her face, "but he says the dirt tastes very bad."

Two weeks later, there is a violent storm. No rain or hail or thunder or lightning. Just a screaming wind. Nature is sharpening its teeth. We crowd in front of the TV and watch footage of gray tornadoes crossing highways, hunting for something to uproot.

. . .

The twins inform us that they're moving on. They want to see more of this world while they still can. They've heard the Koreshan State Historic Site in Estero has been reactivated. The last members deeded the land to the state in the sixties, but in recent weeks people have taken it back. The new Koreshans have the trees that were originally imported from Australia and Africa, log cabins, a political action committee, an orange grove, canoes. "We've always been very spiritual," the twins tell us. "Also, if we can be honest for a minute, this house is getting a little crowded." My mother seems relieved by their announcement. In recent days, the twins have become a hectoring presence at her meetings. At the bus station, my mother offers them sleeping bags and sacks of dried beans. On the way home, she drives and my sister sits in the passenger seat. At a red light, my sister bursts into tears and shouts at my mother to pull over. She opens the door, vomits onto the emergency lane, and then tells my mother that she's pregnant. "Oh, honey," our mother says. In an instant, I see the cult leader recede, the retired social worker step forward. She runs around to the passenger side and pops open the glove compartment. She finds a crumpled paper napkin and dabs at my sister's face.

This is going to sound really strange, my sister texts me a few nights later. *But I think something about my vision has changed. I think I can see in the dark?*

. . .

One night, I sneak into a community pool to run an experiment. My husband comes with me, to operate as a lookout and also to record the time. I slide into the pool and paddle out into the deep end. I tell him that I'm going to dive under and that he is not to come after me, no matter how long I stay down there. I gather oxygen deep into my lungs and plunge.

Underwater time moves at a different pace. The world down here is full of dead leaves and wavering shadows. A plastic baby doll with a missing arm languishes at the bottom, her hair stuck in the drain. I notice an air bubble forming on the tip of my nose, like a large bead of sweat. I watch with fascination as it expands and contracts. My mouth is closed and water is not flowing into my nostrils. Still, somehow, I am able to breathe.

The air bubble bursts. I feel a tremendous pressure in my chest. After I break through the surface, my husband tells me that I stayed under for twenty-two minutes.

Whenever my sister and I expressed grievances as children, our mother would say that we should count our blessings that we're not ants, who spend their entire lives moving dirt from one pile to another. But an ant, an insect, a common reptile—maybe now that is exactly what we should hope to become.

I keep building my Florida Diary. I keep writing down ideas about the world, from both my own imagination and the imaginations of others. Like these snippets from a book I read on time. 1. A position in time is called a moment. 2. Time involves change; a universe in which nothing changes would be a timeless universe. 3. An event can never cease to be an event. 4. Whenever we judge anything to exist in time we are in error. And when we perceive anything as existing in time—the only way in which we ever do perceive things—we are perceiving it more or less as it really is not. 5. Perhaps time is ultimate, which is to say it is not a thing that can be explained, nor is an explanation required.

The more I read, the more, and the less, I understand.

One of the weirdest things about this period of time is the parts that still seem normal. Mundane and non-apocalyptic. Like how one minute we need an inflatable raft to cross the street and another we're eating pasta at my sister's house and she's sitting back in her chair, one hand on her melon of a belly, and telling a story about how her neighbor bit someone in the face at Oktoberfest last year. *I mean, the other guy called his wife a twat, right in front of everyone at Oktoberfest, and, well, that was one way to handle it* . . .

That old world still exists, is what I mean. Distant, but not forgotten. No, no. We will never forget all those good times. Now that world is like an old friend who comes to visit on occasion, but who can never stay for too long.

Acknowledgments

Page 139 contains quotes from Anne Carson's "The Anthropology of Water."

Page 208 contains quotes from "The Unreality of Time" by J.M.E. McTaggart.

To my family, first and foremost. The years we unexpectedly got to spend together were transformative and I miss you all every day.

To Katherine Fausset: thank you for always believing in me. To Jackson Howard: I am so excited to be on this journey with you. All my gratitude to Mitzi Angel, Jenna Johnson, and Sean McDonald for your support. Thanks also to Brianna Fairman, Brian Gittis, Debra Helfand, Na Kim, Bri Panzica, Lisa Silverman, Caitlin Van Dusen, and Greg Villepique.

To my early readers, Sarah and Jami: thank you for your guidance. To Elliott and Lauren: thank you for your friendship and for the steady and inspired reminders of why art matters. To Mike and Shuchi: for always being down to talk on the phone. Thank you to everyone at Elite Boxing in Oviedo for the community and for helping me find my strength. The next book is for y'all. To Oscar: thank you for being my faithful writing companion.

This book owes a massive debt to the John Simon Guggenheim Memorial Foundation, the American Academy of Arts and Letters, and the National Endowment for the Arts. Thank you for the time to dream, and for the chance to go home.

To Paul: thank you for letting me use your stories about the exceptional strangeness witnessed on your marathon runs. This book started with your willingness to donate material to the cause. Every day you make me so glad that I'm still here.

A NOTE ABOUT THE AUTHOR

Laura van den Berg was born and raised in Florida. She is the author of the story collections *What the World Will Look Like When All the Water Leaves Us*, *The Isle of Youth*, and *I Hold a Wolf by the Ears*, which was named one of the ten best fiction books of 2020 by *Time*, and the novels *Find Me* and *The Third Hotel*, which was a finalist for the New York Public Library Young Lions Fiction Award, was an Indie Next pick, and was named a best book of 2018 by more than a dozen publications. She is the recipient of a Guggenheim Fellowship, a Strauss Living Award and a Rosenthal Family Foundation Award from the American Academy of Arts and Letters, a literature fellowship from the National Endowment for the Arts, the Bard Fiction Prize, a PEN/O. Henry Prize, and a MacDowell Fellowship, and she is a two-time finalist for the Frank O'Connor International Short Story Award. She is currently a senior lecturer on fiction at Harvard University. She lives in the Hudson Valley.